Widow's Walk

Widow's Walk

Andrew Coburn

Five Star
Unity, Maine

This novel is a work of fiction. Names, characters, places, and incidents are either the product of the author's imagination, or, if real, used fictitiously.

Five Star First Edition Mystery Series.
Published in 2001 in conjunction with
Tekno Books and Ed Gorman.

Cover photograph by Tom Kobloch.
Cover design by Carol Pringle.

The text of this edition is unabridged.

Set in 11 pt. Plantin by Elena Picard.

Printed in the United States on permanent paper.

Library of Congress Cataloging-in-Publication Data

Coburn, Andrew.
  Widow's walk / by Andrew Coburn.
    p. cm.
  ISBN 0-7862-3160-2 (hc : alk. paper)
  1. Police—New Hampshire—Fiction. 2. Serial murders
—Fiction. 3. Police chiefs—Fiction. 4. New Hampshire
—Fiction. I. Title.
PS3553.O23 W54 2001
813'.54—dc21   2001018149

For Joseph Shellenbach and Gretchen Ryder

"When a man abuses a woman, he's trying to hide the fact he's scarcely a man."
—Joseph Shellenbach

One

The tide was scuttling in. Pebbles dribbled onto the drenched sand, and the cool reached her skin, salting it. From her low beach chair, she said, "I know what you're doing behind those goggles."

The dentist swiftly shifted his gaze from slim adolescent beauties at the water's edge. He stood with his hands on his hips, his black trunks so sleek he looked oiled around the middle. He had not been in the water yet, and his baked shoulders smelled of Coppertone, his underarms of Yardley soap. Blondish and middle-aged, masked in Polaroid sunglasses, he managed to make his soft body seem tough through stomach suction and bursts of punishing exercise. Half under his breath, he said, "Come off it, Cora."

"I'm not stupid."

"I'm doing absolutely nothing."

"Really."

"Really!" he said. The adolescent girls had crashed into the surf.

"Then I'll leave you to it," she said coldly and uprooted herself from the tiny chair as jet aircraft from Pease Air Force Base rumbled on the New Hampshire horizon.

"Cora."

She did not look back. A sunburned man, parts of him peeling, rose massively from a blanket and blocked the dentist's view.

"Your chair!"

He wanted her to take it with her, but she ignored him. She angled past children molding castles and lowered her head as the bombers' roar consumed the sky. She detoured to the left, out of the way of Winnie Wallace, a real estate agent, who lay face-down and spread out with closed eyes and loose straps, and she steered clear of the noisy Farnham family, with whom she was not friendly.

Each step was strenuous, her small sandaled feet carrying the weight of packed thighs through shimmers of heat. Boys scuffing sand shied away from her. The expression on her tight face suggested a woman easily piqued, and her manner left little doubt. Her sprayed and blackened hair was shaped into a tall tube that from afar resembled a horn or a hunk of iron. Each night she washed her hair, got all the stick out, and let it dry loose and witch-like in the event her husband wanted her. Each morning she spent an hour restructuring it.

Three women noted her departure.

Vivid creatures of perfect tooth and agreeable looks, they stood silhouetted on the porch of the gray beachfront house they were renting for the season. The tallest, a tumbler of iced tea in her hand, contracted her eyelids and nudged the wheat-haired woman next to her.

"Is that his wife?"

"I can't imagine it being anybody else's."

The third woman stirred, as if from a twinge. "It's not hard to guess what she puts up with," she murmured, winsome in a white sleeveless robe that clung to her. The robe pulled apart as she inched from the rail. "Who's going down to the water?"

Somebody else noticed the dentist's wife's departure.

He was Police Chief Paul Jenkins, whose presence on the beach was a friendly reminder of the ban on alcoholic beverages, loud radios, and loose dogs. A lick of light hair stuck to his moist forehead. His face was lean and comfortably lined, and his nose was thin, a blade. He had on a loose-hanging shirt, chino pants, and soiled desert boots. No badge showing, none needed. Most residents of Boar's Bluff, including seasonal ones, knew him by sight.

Had the dentist's wife looked his way, he'd have waved.

She saw none of them or, if she did, gave no sign. She followed the short private road that led from the beach to Ocean Boulevard. Lips compressed, she waited for a break in the hot traffic, which did not come. Her face turned juicy in the heat. She counted, as usual, more Massachusetts cars than New Hampshire ones, which annoyed her. Outlanders. Three motorcyclists bent over the handles hammered by, which annoyed her more. Low life. Disregardful of the traffic, she crossed Ocean Boulevard.

Horns blasted at her.

Adjusting the towel, fixing it into a poncho, she entered Philpott's store and purchased hair spray, aspirin, Rolaids, and Trident sugarless gum. "Charge it," she said and ambled by a rack of magazines to the snack bar, breakfasts and lunches, the best hamburgers in town, the worst coffee. She was not in the least surprised to see her brother nursing the remains of a milkshake. Corner stool. Jobless, he spent half his time there. She took the swivel seat beside him, and he turned to her, showing a large complacent face.

"Are you very busy, Bud?"

"Is that supposed to be funny?" He spoke with a certain absence of life, as though vital parts of him had been short-circuited. He was her younger brother and a mistake in her mother's life. She, not her late mother, had assumed the umbilical role.

"Do me a favor," she said and watched him return his eyes to the shake glass. Though going unpleasantly bald, he still bore traces of his boyish looks. "Take a walk near the beach, but don't let Stephen see you."

He raised his head and seemed to peer at her through layers of light. His sigh was deep.

"Nothing, dear," she said abruptly, waving off the girl working the counter. Then she smiled thinly at her brother. "Isn't it odd I never get an argument when I give you money, only when I want something in return?"

His large lips barely moved. "Get off my ass."

"Of course. Forever, if you like."

His shoulders sagged, as if air were seeping out. He spoke into the glass. "You always get what you want, don't you?"

She reached past him and ripped a napkin from a container, then blew her nose. "None of us gets everything. Remember that, Bud."

"I will."

She watched him leave.

The dentist woke in the moonlit dim of night and found his wife peering at him, her knees dug into the mattress. Her rump rested on her heels, and her hands lay loose on thighs that, flattened out, had doubled in size. Even with her wild flood of hair and her nakedness in the sequined nightie, she looked prim and righteous. She had the air of a hardened churchgoer, though she was not one. Startled, he said, "What are you doing?"

"Just for the record, tell me."

"Tell you *what?*"

She billowed forward on her knees, her face expanding out of the hair. Her long fingernails looked capable of ripping him from scrotum to throat. "How many women have there been?"

"I've never cheated on you, Cora."

"I don't believe you."

"Maybe once."

"Maybe twice," she said, mocking his tone.

"All right, maybe twice, maybe three times."

"Maybe four."

"Maybe never. Did you ever think of that?"

"You're cute, Stephen." The voice was frigid. "Very cute."

His head twitched on the pillow. "Cora, lie down."

She arched her back. "Again for the record, who is it this time? One of the sluts renting the gray house?"

"In your mind, who isn't a slut? Will you please be sensible!"

"You were seen." Her voice turned smug and in a bitter way triumphant. "Have you dumped Winnie Wallace?"

A floral sheet covered him. He flipped it off, angry that she had robbed him of the sweetness of sleep, which he knew would not return easily. He swung his legs forcefully over the side.

"Where are you going?"

"I can't sleep now, that's for sure." He rattled open a drawer in the half-light, slipped on a jockstrap, and fumbled for the pieces of his gray sweatsuit.

"Nothing's settled."

"It never is."

"She might not let you off the hook."

His head popped out of the top of the sweatshirt. He cinched the pants. "What are you saying now?"

"Winnie. She's the vindictive type."

"You should talk." He put on socks and official track shoes, and raced a comb through his hair.

"So you're going for a run."

"Do you mind?"

"It won't solve anything."

"For a while it will," he said and left.

The night was warm, almost clammy. Except for a patch of light here and there or the fruity glow of a color TV, the houses were dark. A dog barked, then another, and he quickened his pace. Unlike his swimming stroke, his stride was not smooth.

As he crossed Ocean Boulevard against the distant glare of headlamps, the moonlight faded, clouds rushed in. By the time he reached the void of the nighttime beach, the darkness was complete. The beach was off-limits after midnight, but usually somebody or other was on it, so he was not surprised when he heard the vague voices of youths and the distinct laughter of a girl. Much farther away a car door banged. Then he began chugging hard, punishing his body, and heard only his own breathing and the sea rushing over itself. He didn't stop until he reached the bend in the beach, where boulders glistened through the dark. Panting heavily, he stood for a number of moments with his head lowered, his hands on his knees. When he straightened he saw the sudden pulse of a cigarette.

He walked toward it.

Hetty Nelson, an elderly woman who regularly combed the beach at the crack of dawn, thought he was asleep and was about to poke him with a stick. Then she saw his face.

Two

A smile seemed to protrude from the lips, as though the dentist were voluptuously aware of his death. The wound was a puckered hole in the blond head of hair, with most of the blood soaked into the sand, a small but deep stain. Nearby a gull screeched. Edging away from his sergeant, Chief Paul Jenkins went behind a boulder, pointed his face at the silence of the sand, and retched.

The sergeant pretended not to notice. He glanced over his shoulder toward the border of the beach. Only a small crowd had gathered because the hour was still early. Hetty Nelson, the old thing who lived year-round in the pink cottage next to the gray house, sat on a bleached log halfway up the sand. She had been told to return to her cottage, but the log was as far as she had gone.

The chief emerged from behind the boulder and was as pale as the sergeant had ever seen him. The chief moved toward the sea and stopped at the edge, where he removed his desert boots and socks and rolled his pant-legs to the knees. Then he waded into the water and rinsed his mouth, splashed his face, and slicked his hair. The sergeant called out.

"Chief, come on back. People are watching."

The chief took his time, shook his feet, dried them as well as he could, and unraveled his pant-legs. Struggling with a sock, he glimpsed a washed-up starfish, brain-pink and dog-eared, and considered scooping it up for Hetty Nelson, though she doubtlessly had hundreds. She was a collector, some said a scavenger, and her cottage stank of the stuff.

"You all right, Chief?"

The chief nodded, no longer pale but faintly flushed.

The sergeant—his name was Wilbur Cox—wore the gray-green uniform of the Boar's Bluff Police Department, the lightweight cap squarely on his head. Stout arms hung from the starched cuffs of the short-sleeved shirt probably done up that morning by his wife. His voice had a blunt edge. "He wasn't that good a friend of yours, was he?"

"He wasn't a friend at all."

"That's what I mean. He wasn't even your dentist, was he?"

"That's right, Wilbur. He wasn't."

The sergeant took a deep breath, his chest expanding. "I don't mind telling you, I'm excited. Our first murder."

"Assuming that's what it is."

"I know a bullet wound when I see one, Chief."

"How many have you seen?"

The sergeant stiffened. He was a veteran of Vietnam, the chief of Korea. The sergeant had returned to Boar's Bluff with a major medal for bravery, the chief with a slight limp. He had fallen off a truck. The sergeant said, "Probably more than you."

The chief squinted at the sky and then at the surf. The ocean tones were distinct, blues competing with greens. The waves were milky. The sergeant grew restless, as if he had a role to play, a brief to follow, and the chief was holding him back.

"I guess we don't want to just stand here, Chief. That crowd's going to grow."

The chief tested his legs. They didn't seem steady. "You go find a telephone. I'll stay."

"Right." The sergeant hesitated. "Who am I calling?"

"Who else? The state police."

The sergeant looked disappointed. "It's still going to be our case, isn't it?"

"Teamwork, Wilbur."

"Right." Again he hesitated. "I was thinking, while I'm at it, how about the media? I mean, why not—huh?"

"We'll wait on that."

"Okay. How about the medical examiner?"

"Yes. Quincy, if you can get him."

The sergeant didn't smile.

Uncomfortably alone with the body, the chief felt like a fisherman guarding his monstrous catch. He looked down at the eyes and at the open lips, a valuable mouth, gold in it. For an unsettling second he feared the dentist might sit up and barter for his life.

From the distance of the bleached log, Hetty Nelson smiled at him. She stretched out her thin legs and crossed them at the ankles. Her body was still dependable, but no one was sure about her mind. She smiled again, patiently, as if she had a claim on the corpse.

Winnie Wallace lived in an attractive house near the bluff for which the town was named. Sober-faced, she carried a cup of coffee from the kitchen to a distant room that had a picture window and an ocean view. A desk of teak and chrome dominated the room, from which she conducted a real estate business that had grown through the years. The coffee, brewed strong, braced her. She set the cup down and picked up the telephone. She rang up the gray house, which she had rented to three women from Massachusetts and spoke to the one named Joan Weiss.

"I was riding by. What's going on over there?"

"No one knows for sure, but it seems somebody might have drowned. Or something."

"My God. Any idea who?"

"None. No one's allowed on the beach. I've never seen so many police. Mostly state troopers."

"If you hear anything, will you call me?"

"Of course."

Winnie carried her coffee outdoors, away from the shadow of the tall house, a handsomely trim blue-eyed woman who did not fight the silver creeping into her hair. Aqua underpants shaded the thin white of her styled trousers. Standing near a rock, she held her shoulders high and sipped coffee. Later she placed the cup on the rock and proceeded to a prominent point on the bluff, where she gave the ocean a serious stare. At first she ignored the whisper of footsteps behind her. Then she said, "Friend or foe?"

"That's never been clear."

"You muddied the waters, not I."

Chief Paul Jenkins stood beside her, his hands squeezed into the back pockets of his chinos. "You have a short memory."

"Selective," she said, a stray breeze spreading her hair and lifting his. "It's how I survive. With us, Paul, it was a case of stamina. Neither of us had it in those days. Damn, we go back, don't we!"

"A good argument against living out your life in your hometown."

She toed the ground, sand and stone, some grass, and said in a hoarse tone, "We did it just about everywhere. Did we do it here?"

"I think I'd have remembered."

"Yes, I would have, too." She watched him pull his hands from his rear pockets and adjust his rangy stance. His jaw was unshaved. Their eyes so far had not wholly met. Now they did. "Who drowned?"

"No one."

"Thank God."

"But we have an apparent homicide."

"What?"

"Stephen Dray. Sometime after midnight."

Her eyes were cloudy blue, expressionless, though there was a faint twitch at one corner of her lightly painted mouth. "Figures, doesn't it?"

"At the moment nothing figures."

"Cora know?" Her voice was low-pitched.

"Somebody's telling her. My sergeant."

"Wilbur? Wilbur Cox? Jesus, Paul."

"His wife used to clean for her."

"That's worse." Her body seemed to curve away from him, as if she had taken a low punch in the back. "Was he beaten, strangled, what?"

"Shot."

Her eyes roamed restlessly, her profiled face sharply defined. Small birds specked the sky. She followed their flight.

Much seemed to be going on inside her head, and she spoke with a joking nervousness that was like courage. "Are you here to hold my hand, or am I a suspect?"

"I'm here, Win. That's all. I could use a coffee."

She took his arm, and they headed back toward the house. On the way she retrieved her empty cup, dangling it from her little finger. "You have to be careful of me. I'm cool."

"I can see that."

"Surprise you?"

He remembered how they had met, over a spinning bottle at a grade school party. She still had her baby fat, and he was skin and bones, a lank line of poor posture that straightened when he played high school basketball, the team's top scorer until he fouled his knee. She was not a cheerleader, but she was often in the stands, and he was frequently in her school-girl bedroom decorated by movie magazine photos of Farley Granger and Guy Madison. Later she accused him of telling. The accusation was unwarranted. Actually it was her excuse to see somebody else.

His car, an unmarked black Ford, was parked in the drive behind her Honda Civic. The highway, a wide extension of Ocean Boulevard, lay beyond. He watched a small white sports car float like a piece of silk through the heat haze, Portsmouth way. She said, "That's Bud Brown."

"I know who it is."

"He should be with Cora. Doesn't he know?"

"Apparently not."

The car vanished. They entered the house, the kitchen. The chief sat at a butcher's block table, and she, drifting around a counter, looked over her shoulder at him. "Would you rather have a Bloody Mary?" He nodded, and she reached for two glasses. From the distant part of the kitchen, she said, "Do you think I did it?"

"No."

"You might be wrong."

"I know."

With a loud crack, she broke apart ice cubes.

She served him. Strong Bloody Marys. Her knee accidentally brushed his under the table, and he flinched, as if from the old injury. He silently drummed his fingers on the table. "Winnie."

"What?"

"Were you still seeing him?"

She shook her head. "I broke it off some time ago."

"You did?"

She colored slightly. "Maybe it was mutual. Okay?"

He tasted his drink. Hers was already half consumed. He

said, "When's the last time you saw him?"

"You're interrogating me." Her laugh was low, almost inaudible. "Yes, that's exactly what you're doing."

"Call it a dry run, Win. Lieutenant Haas won't be easy on you."

"Who the hell is Lieutenant Haas?"

"More of a policeman than me."

"State?"

"Yes. Detective division."

"Am I supposed to be afraid?"

"No. Simply prepared."

The body had been removed, but the beach remained closed as a uniformed trooper moved over the sand with a metal detector, another with a rake, while others made their slow way among rocks and along the water's edge—soft figures, all of them, in the filtered sunlight. The trooper with the rake glanced roguishly at the one with the detector. "You find any money, it's mine."

A voice from the middle of the beach said, "Keep moving."

Lieutenant Haas. He stood clean-cut and brisk-looking in a blue cord suit, his smooth and skimpy hair impeccably combed and parted, his protuberant eyes moist. His face was long and youngish, dainty in a way, nervous around the nostrils. He was returning from a long talk with the old woman, Hetty Nelson, and wondering whether he had wasted his time. Something in the back of his skull told him he hadn't. He turned around at the approach of the local sergeant, Wilbur Cox.

"How'd she take it?"

Sergeant Cox shrugged. "Like a cold fish."

"Interesting."

"No, that's Cora. My wife used to work for her. Never shows anything except to let you know she's ten times better than you."

"That's a way of defense."

"What?"

"The dentist. He liked the ladies?"

The sergeant nodded. "How'd you know?"

"I want a list of them. Can you help me?"

The sergeant rose a little on his toes, taken by a sense of importance and then by a few quick thoughts, which pleased him in a strangely chilling way. Unconsciously he smoothed a palm over his sidearm, a pearl-handled thirty-eight. "Maybe," he said.

"Check with your chief if you're worried."

"I'm not worried."

"Good." Lieutenant Haas cast a backward glance at his troopers and at the wavy line of the ocean. "By the way, where is he?"

The sergeant shook his head. "Don't know."

"Wasn't he with you?"

"No."

"And you don't know where he went?"

The sergeant was silent, at slight odds with himself. His wide face lacked an expression, like that of a gambler with a wild card up his sleeve, perhaps without the nerve to play it. He was still palming his sidearm. Lieutenant Haas looked down.

"Ever fire that at anybody?"

"Not yet."

"You're an optimist," Lieutenant Haas said with the vaguest sort of smile. His watery gaze shifted to the cottages and houses fronting the beach. He pointed. "Who lives in those cottages there, the white ones, not the pink one."

"Summer residents, out-of-state."

Lieutenant Haas's necktie was silk. He fingered it. "And the gray house?"

"More of the same. Three women from Boston. They're new."

"Shall we?"

"You mean, see if anybody saw or heard anything? I was going to do that. I was waiting for the chief."

"We don't want to wait too long, do we?"

"No, sir."

They walked measuredly, tilted forward. Swiftly the heat of the day became more apparent. The sergeant swayed, tugged at his cap and spoke suddenly. "Lieutenant."

They stopped. Lieutenant Haas waited.

"Can I talk to you in confidence?" The voice was scratchy, the tone almost obsequious. "It's about the chief."

Lieutenant Haas was taller than the sergeant. He lowered his head. "Of course you can."

Three

Chief Jenkins swerved onto Lodge Road in the unmarked and unwashed Ford, the right rear tire in need of air, and a moment later parked in front of a house with an unregistered VW camper in the drive. Charlene, the oldest of the five Farnham children, sat on the side steps with her knees drawn up under her chin. The chief stayed in his car, waiting for her to acknowledge his presence. "You want something," she finally called out, and he nodded. She came forward in a loaded Mickey Mouse T-shirt and denim shorts pinched into her crotch. She was barely sixteen. "It's about him, isn't it?" she said with some defiance, and the chief again nodded.

"I know he was your friend."

"You think you know everything." She took a short breath. "Somebody said he was drowned. Then somebody else said he was murdered."

"We're not sure yet."

Legs suddenly quivering, she stepped close to the Ford and rested a hand on the door for support.

"Relax," he said. There was, he felt, a trust between them, established a summer ago in the evening dim behind the high school, a boy on her, a bit of a dullard moving furiously as if to hammer her flat. He could have run them in, not for the sexual mischief which he deemed none of his business but for the plastic packets spilling from a tote bag, more than enough to charge them with pushing as well as using. He gave them a break by emptying the packets and scattering the evidence.

When the boy tried to slink away, the chief drilled two fingers down the back of his collar and warned them both. *Next time no!*

She said, "If he was drowned, you'd know that right away, wouldn't you?"

"Not necessarily." The chief was being both mysterious and avuncular. "When did you see him last?"

Her mouth trembled. "Don't make me into a pig."

He felt vaguely like a bully but not enough to let her alone. "You were in his car a couple of times, the Cadillac, isn't that true?"

"Nothing happened!"

She verged on tears, and for an instant the chief hated himself, for the girl, despite her physical maturity, was still a child and far from the brightest of her classmates. "Were you on the beach last night? I'm only interested in what you might have seen or heard."

"I wasn't there."

"Maybe with some of your friends."

"No," she said, and the tears came. A black dog appeared, as if to protect her. She reached blindly to stroke its head.

"I'm not going to talk to your parents, if that's what you're worried about."

She pushed the dog away. "Can I go?"

The chief seemed to nod.

She took three self-conscious steps and wheeled around. "I don't owe you my life, you know!"

"You don't owe me anything," he said and drove away.

It grew dark. Hetty Nelson kept the cottage door open to let the moonlight slant in, her way of saving electricity and airing out the place. The skeletal remains of a crab, legs intact, glinted dully from a windowsill, as if it had crawled there from the box it belonged in. She sidestepped netting from a shattered lobster trap, broken ribs and rusty nails entangled in it, and wound the kitchen clock. The hour was late only for her. Her eyes were hooded, the wrinkled lids resembling walnut shells. She took aspirin for her arthritis. She was eighty-seven years old. She let out a jaw-creaking yawn and looked like a baby bird, just born.

In the black of her bedroom, scarcely bigger than a walk-in closet, she scratched inside her shirt, between baked-apple breasts, and muttered to herself, something about the dentist. Her bent fingers had problems with buttons, and she was slow to undress. Her cotton nightgown was under the pillow. She slipped the bedraggled gown over her head and was smoothing it down when a large pair of hands gripped her throat from behind. Her eyes rolled.

"You silly boy."

She was not allowed to turn around. That was the rule of the game initiated by the man when he was a boy running her errands and visiting her in the night, sneaking in to surprise her, to scare her if possible. Even then he was an insomniac. A swollen figure of a boy chewing her stale cookies and pawing into her sand dollars and snail shells, pocketing the choice ones. The odd thing was that she had never much liked him, but she had craved company—and his had grown on her. The visits, which he had kept secret from his sister, had been frequent. Now they were occasional, though still secret. He whispered, "Guess who?"

She struggled a little, also part of the game. "It must be Bud."

His fingers kneaded the hatched skin and struck cords, not hard enough to hurt her. He swayed against her.

"Don't do that," she said. "I don't like it." He had broken a rule, and she was vaguely uneasy. "That's enough. Let me go." She added, "Your sister shouldn't be alone."

"People are with her." He still spoke in a whisper, a rough one, well above her head. "From the church."

"Bud." She could smell his breath. He'd been sucking sweets. "Did you kill him?"

"No," he said, and she felt him freeze.

"Did Cora? Don't lie."

He was silent. His hands fell from her shoulders. She took her time turning around, unable to see. She was not even sure he was still there until she spotted the whites of his eyes.

"Who then? You can tell me."

"I only know it wasn't me. But they might think it was."

She could see better now. A part of his face loomed up. "They think that, then they can talk to me. I'll tell 'em you're a good boy."

"I'm a man."

"You go to Cora," she said with sudden fatigue that affected her voice. "She'll watch out for you. I'm too old."

Her words went unheard.

She lifted her head and, seeing that he was gone, said, "Good, Bud. Good boy." Then she flexed her neck, as if still feeling his hands around it.

Chief Jenkins, cruising Ocean Boulevard, saw Bud Brown's car in Philpott's lighted lot. He did not see Bud Brown. Nor did he see him inside when he drifted close to the store. He turned onto Lodge Road and soon approached the dentist's house, a few cars in front. He considered stopping but didn't.

Away from the coast the town swiftly turned rural—woods, stone walls, fields, farm houses, here and there an orchard, a farm (once he had plowed into a pig straying across the road in the dead of night), all roads meandering to Route

One. Using a shortcut, he reached Route One in ten minutes, passed Skelly's Mobil, which was closing, and pulled up at a pizza place flaming with neon. At the entrance he stepped aside for departing youths, louts wearing leather despite the evening heat. Inside he sat at a table and ordered coffee from a waitress he didn't know. She was new, probably from another town, most likely Hampton or Seabrook. He said, "Where's Gladys?"

"Who?" Her face was small and worn, and her hair was damp where it touched her skin.

"Gladys Cox."

"Oh, you mean the cop's wife. She only works weekends now. Her kids were giving her trouble. You got kids?"

The chief shook his head.

"You're lucky. I've got three teenage turds. I told her wait till hers get that age. That's your real trouble."

The chief, rising, said, "Skip the coffee."

She looked at him speculatively. "You fooling around with her? If you are I'm glad. I don't think much of her husband."

Winnie Wallace placed a call to the other side of town. She had tried several times before and this time was successful. A man answered, which was lucky. Usually his wife did.

"Lyman."

"Yes," he said, and his brusque manner threw her off, though it should not have. Part of the settlement, years ago, was that she would not in any way disturb his life.

"Lyman." Her voice was strained, and she was not sure he recognized it. "It's Winnie."

"I know who it is."

"Can Amy hear?"

"She went out to dinner with her father. She'll be home

soon." His impatience came through. "What do you want, Winnie?"

"Please come over. I need somebody to talk to."

"It's not possible."

"Lyman, please. I don't want to be alone."

"I heard about the dentist," he said. "Don't get me involved."

"I'm scared," she said, shivering. "It's hit me all at once."

The silence from the other end seemed to throb in her ear.

"Don't hang up," she said.

But he did.

At times Bud Brown moved trance-like along Ocean Boulevard; at other times he did not move at all. He was away from the cottages and near large lighted houses with widow's walks and dogs he didn't know. He avoided them. When a man taking out rubbish peered at him, he froze. He thought it was the dentist.

He crossed the boulevard and reversed his course, passing a lighthouse that had been redesigned into a home, its shape wrenched into uneven cubes shooting out shadows in odd directions. Pinkish fluorescent light leaked out at the top, an easy climb but not tonight. His heart was not in it. His world seemed divided and re-divided, and he did not know which patch was safe. When a pickup truck riding high on oversized tires slashed him with its lights, he veered onto grass and hastened his pace.

Philpott's was about to close. It closed at eleven. People were cleaning up and counting cash, and the parking lot, where Bud Brown had left his car, was already dark. The six-year-old Corvette, a sheen of silvery white, lay ahead. It was his polished jewel, nearly a love object. As he reached for the door handle, he gave a start. Somebody was sitting inside. A voice came out the open window.

"I've been waiting for you."

Bud Brown pulled back and did a foolish thing. He ran.

Chief Jenkins did not give chase. He couldn't have caught him anyway, and with a sigh he pulled himself out of the Corvette, locking it to discourage theft. He knew how much it was prized. His own car, the Ford, was parked across the boulevard and he plodded toward it in his quiet well-worn desert boots. With each step he felt the dampness of the sea in his trick knee. Over the years the ache had become almost pleasant.

He drove along a dark byway through a wooded area that was marshy in sections, peepers roaring. He accelerated, knowing he shouldn't. The Ford rattled and pitched. Soon he saw a house shedding light through the trees. The house, which was small, four square rooms and a porch enclosed by latticework, was his and should have been dark. No car was in the drive. He parked under a pine.

He smelled brewed coffee. An owl hooted, a friend of sorts, the droppings perpetual presents. As a boy he'd been taught you could learn much about an owl from its pellets. He mounted footworn porch steps and entered his house. Winnie Wallace was in the kitchen, standing slackly with a mug of coffee in one hand and a cigarette in the other.

"Don't be mad," she said.

He was annoyed. "How'd you get in?"

"It didn't take much to find the key." She butted out the cigarette in the saucer she'd been using as an ashtray and stood provocatively, the graying head of hair appealingly curly, the eyes baby-doll blue. "You *are* mad."

"Where's your car?"

"I took a taxi. Didn't want you sending me home." Her

laugh was jerky, and she spilled coffee. The blue of her eyes seemed drained. "Sorry. I get giddy when I'm nervous."

"What are you nervous about?"

"A man is dead."

"If you didn't do it, why be scared?"

"Now you're not sure."

"I'm sure," he said, noticing that her lips were dry to the point of cracking. "That's going to stain."

"It's my shirt."

He went into the bathroom and for a while stared at the shower curtain, turning over too many thoughts to concentrate on one. He placed his face near the open window for the breeze. The owl had changed trees. He could tell by the hoot. A minute later he flushed the john, though he had not used it. When he came out, she was in the bedroom staring at the bed. She seemed baffled.

"What's the matter?"

"Which side is mine?"

Four

The police station, a mile from Ocean Boulevard, occupied the first-floor rear of the Town Hall. Alice Cross, a civilian, worked the police desk, which included the radio (surplus equipment from Pease) and the log that she maintained in exquisite penmanship. She was sipping her second cup of coffee when Sergeant Wilbur Cox stuck his head out of the chief's office.

"Call him. Tell him we're waiting."

There were two ways of telling a person to do something, and her look said she didn't care for his. She knew he was showing off in front of the lieutenant from the state police and using the chief's desk as if it were his own. She lifted the telephone and buttoned a number, surprised when a woman answered and angry when she recognized the voice.

"We overslept," Winnie Wallace said with a certain satisfaction.

"Is he on his way?"

"Soon. How are you, Alice?"

"Busy."

A few minutes later Sergeant Cox reappeared without her noticing and stood behind her, his thumbs hooked on the burnished leather of his wide belt. She was sipping her coffee abstractedly, unconsciously pulling a face each time she raised the cup. His voice startled her: "Well?"

She spun in her chair. "Don't do that!"

"What's the matter, Alice? Got a hair across your ass?"

Had she been standing she might have slapped his face. She neither liked nor trusted him and never had, her attitude forged when he was a teenager and one of several toughs suspected of torching a stable and beheading a horse. His police appointment was in recognition of his military service, bolstered by the fact that at the time he was the only applicant. She had advised the chief against the appointment and later had rendered the same sentiment against his promotion.

"When's he coming?"

"When he gets here."

"Did you tell him how long we've been waiting?"

"Maybe, Wilbur, he doesn't care."

"Maybe he had a real rough night. That could be."

Alice said nothing, hoping the sergeant knew no more than he should.

The wife of the Episcopal minister stayed the night at the home of Cora Dray, who, despite sedatives, slept little. In the morning, the minister's wife looked in on her and said, "Let me get you breakfast."

Cora sat against a propped pillow, the covers smoothed around her waist, her head high and her hair coiled, undisturbed. The shades were pulled, and in the half-light she seemed dumb and sightless. Rousing herself, she said, "No, nothing." The voice was dull. "Is my brother here?"

"No."

"Poor Bud, bald before his time. He was as fair, you know, as I was dark. People used to comment on that."

"Would you like me to telephone him?"

"He doesn't have a phone. When people want him, they call here. They think this is his home." Her sigh was imperceptible. "He doesn't have much of anything, really. Except that car, of course."

31

"It was a generous gift."

"Stephen's." The voice had an edge. "Not mine." Cora raised her eyes. "I want Stephen cremated."

"Are you sure, Cora?" The other woman spoke in a strained whisper. "His . . . his body was so important to him."

"Cremation and a private service. Bud and I will be the only ones there. And, of course, your husband."

The minister's wife, an immobile figure, spoke from a small cut of a mouth. "Do you want me there?"

"It's up to you," Cora said and sought to sit straight. The minister's wife immediately went to her aid rearranging the pillows. Cora smiled chillingly. "You look quite charming in my robe. Of course that's not all you used of mine, is it, dear?"

The minister's wife jerked back, stung by the words. The skin under her eyes and at her jawline was unnaturally tight from cosmetic surgery.

"Did you think I was stupid?" Cora said and closed her eyes.

The morning regulars at the snack bar in Philpott's hunched over their coffee and muffins and spoke in confidential tones about the death of the dentist. A man wearing work pants bitten at the ankles by bicycle clips said, "I heard he wasn't all that wet, so he damn well didn't drown."

"You can drown in a puddle."

"You can drown drinking too much water," a third man said with a slight rattle: dentures. "I read of a kid that did that."

A fourth man said, "My wife's sure it was a heart attack from too much of you know what."

"That don't hurt you," said the man wearing the clips,

though he was not a cyclist. He drove a soft-drinks truck. "My doctor says it keeps you in shape, like pushups."

The men fell silent when a woman buying butter and eggs hesitated near them. They were aging natives of the town and all had flabby faces bearing no traces of their younger selves. At one time or another, each had worked for Ed Robertshaw, either at his farm or his orchard or for his construction company, which repaired highways for the state, some of the work said to be phantom. When the woman moved away, the one with the rattle said, "I heard he looked killed."

"Where'd you hear that?"

"Hetty Nelson was telling people. She said she thought he was asleep and was gonna hit him with a stick."

"How'd he look killed?"

"She didn't say."

"Maybe," said the man with the bicycle clips, "she did hit him with a stick, and that's what killed him."

"Can you imagine Chief Jenkins arresting her?"

"I can't imagine the chief arresting anybody. He'd make her promise not to do it again."

The man with the loose dentures said, "I'll tell you somebody the chief should've put away a long time ago."

"Who's that?"

"Who d'you think? Bud Brown. That's who Hetty should've hit with a stick, run it right up his ass."

A muscle quivered in Alice Cross's face when Chief Jenkins entered the station. She was gruffly handsome except under the chin where the ruined flesh gave away her age, sixty-five. The chief greeted her warmly and ignored her cold return, having anticipated it. His coffee cup was not in sight. He had anticipated that too. "Ed Robertshaw phoned," she said crisply. "He doesn't know where he'll be, so he'll get back to you."

"How'd he sound?"

"Businesslike."

"Like you."

She turned her back, and he proceeded into his office, nodding to the two men occupying it. They sat to the left of his desk, Sergeant Wilbur Cox with his shoulders squared. Lieutenant Haas rose easily, his fair hair wet-combed and flattened, his eyeballs prominent. He and the chief knew each other faintly. They shook hands.

"It's been awhile."

The chief settled behind his desk, noting that the calendar pad and pencil jar had been disturbed. A pen was missing, his favorite. Pushed to one side was the small leather-framed photograph of a young woman who no longer existed. With a deliberate hand, the chief repositioned it and said, "What did the medical examiner find?"

"A bullet," Lieutenant Haas said. "Twenty-two caliber."

The chief smiled dryly at Sergeant Cox. "You were right, Wilbur."

"Right on the button," the sergeant said, clearly proud of himself. "I was on the news last night, Channel Nine. They were looking for you, but you weren't around."

"I'm glad you were."

"Jim Bartlett interviewed me, a fair guy. I said we hadn't determined the cause of death yet but were working on it with Lieutenant Haas here. The lieutenant was there beside me."

"That's good, Wilbur. Nothing's real anymore unless it's televised."

Lieutenant Haas said, "Any ideas, Chief?"

The question was tossed out much too casually, and the chief said nothing.

The lieutenant said, "In cases like this we usually look

within the family. Sergeant Cox has filled me in on the wife and brother-in-law. We'll also be interested in questioning the victim's friends." The lieutenant smiled vaguely, lips bowed. "I'm referring to his ladies. The sergeant says he had a few."

"He had that reputation," the chief allowed.

Sergeant Cox said, "He was a whoremaster, that's what he was."

"That's why I asked the sergeant to draw up a list of the ladies," Lieutenant Haas went on, and Sergeant Cox, on cue, produced a yellow sheet of paper. He leaned forward and slid it sideways across the desk. It bore more than a dozen names printed in a heavy hand, black ballpoint. The chief eyed it without touching it. After a while he shrugged.

"Most of these are ancient history."

"Then perhaps," Lieutenant Haas offered, "we can safely cross those off. Are there any we might have missed?"

"It's possible."

Lieutenant Haas studied the static image of the chief's face. "Feel free to add on," he said, but the chief did not react.

Sergeant Cox said, "I might have forgotten one. Do I have Winnie Wallace down there?"

The chief looked at the lieutenant. "Are you trying to set me up?" His eyes shifted. "Are you helping him, Wilbur?"

"No one wants to embarrass you," Lieutenant Haas said, touching his silk tie, a shade different from the one worn yesterday.

"You're doing pretty well."

"She was, wasn't she, the victim's last lady?"

"You'll have to ask her that."

Lieutenant Haas's high forehead gave off a bone-like sheen. "Where do we find her, Chief? Her place or yours?"

35

★ ★ ★ ★ ★

He was alone. Alice looked in on him. He said, "I suppose you listened."

She leaned against the doorframe. "I know you get lonely. I understand that." She felt free to talk to him in such a way. They each had had human losses. "Other things I don't understand."

"You worry too much."

"With reason," she said. She had weak arms, and she let them hang as if the life had gone out of them. "I don't know what you're doing—and I'm not sure you do."

"I'm protecting the innocent."

"Good God!" Her face was stricken. "You're not a lawyer. You're supposed to be a policeman." Her mouth pushed at him from across the room, the color flaking off the lips. "And how do you know she's innocent?"

"I *know* Winnie."

"I was afraid you'd say that. Paul, be careful!"

Her eyes were no longer on him but reaching for the framed photograph on his desk. The young woman in the picture, sloe-eyed and full-lipped, had been her daughter and his wife.

Five

Winnie Wallace was no longer at the chief's house, nor was she at her own, where the chief had dropped her off. She was deep in a deck chair on the high porch of the gray house, the visit an impulsive one. Still in yesterday's clothes, the shirt bearing the coffee stain and the styled trousers wrinkled around the hips, she wedged a hand between her legs as children sometimes do. "I hope your party tomorrow will be nice and noisy. It's what I need."

Laura Kimball was sitting upright in a wicker chair. She had been reading and had graciously hidden her annoyance at the interruption. The Patrick White novel lay closed in the lap of her khaki shorts. "With that man dead, I wonder if we should still have it."

"He was nothing to you people."

"We knew him to speak to. He was difficult to avoid."

"He came on strong is what you mean. I know what he was like."

Laura removed her reading glasses and pushed her dark hair back. She had clear eyes, a straight nose, and a way of looking at people that was natural and sincere. With a show of shame, she said, "I'm afraid we made fun of him behind his back. Joan called him a stuffed T-shirt."

"Stuffed jock is what she should've said. He was obsessed with his own body. With him and me, it was purely physical, no pillow talk afterwards, which was okay, since he didn't have anything to say."

Laura seemed shocked. She searched the other's face. "I didn't realize that—"

"Surprise you? Surprised me. I never gave him the time of day till a few months ago. I must've been feeling low."

Gently laying aside the book, a gull feather for a marker, Laura rose on long well-sprung legs and, taller than most women, stood at the rail near a hanging pot of fuchsia. The beach was filling up, families bombarding into view, children running in wild free motions. Joan Weiss, eye-catching in a dusty-pink bathing suit, was at the raw edge of the surf, ready to knife her way into the waves. Pamela Comeau was nearby, wearing the familiar sleeveless robe. Laura suddenly felt uncomfortable with someone she scarcely knew and, turning, said, "Please don't tell me more than you should."

"Am I boring you? I bet I am. Your life's bigger than mine."

Laura was startled.

"It's obvious." Winnie unwedged her hand. "The way the three of you look, act, and talk. You've traveled more, seen more, done more, I can tell. And your men, I'm sure, have been more interesting."

"Why are you selling yourself short?"

"I have an awful taste for the truth."

Laura looked back at the beach and saw only white. With an arid voice, she said, "My life isn't bigger. It may even be smaller."

"Would you trade places?"

"Who knows? I might."

"You'd be foolish. You have more money."

"Why are you so sure?"

"Before you leased this place, I checked your credit. And naturally, your references. Someone called you an activist. I wasn't sure what that meant."

"Years ago I marched. What else do you know about me?"

"Your father was a Unitarian minister, and so was your husband. He left you for another man."

Within, Laura staggered. She placed her cheek against the breath of the beach and mechanically picked charred leaves off the burning fuchsia. "That was some time ago."

"I went too far," Winnie said instantly. "I always do, damn it. I'm sorry."

"You opened a wound."

"I didn't mean to."

"No, I don't think you did," Laura said after a long look, and Winnie squirmed forward in the deck chair, her face lengthening.

"I saw us," she said contritely, "as sisters in suffering. I married young, if you can call it a marriage. His family didn't think I was good enough and broke it up. It was annulled."

"I'm sorry."

"I survived. I was young. Now every change is catastrophic."

Pamela silently appeared on the porch, a humid presence in the white robe, not young enough to be sylph-like but near enough, with a chaste precision to her ice-blond hair. She hovered beside an empty chair, her bathing suit small and smart under the robe. "Am I intruding?"

"No, I am," Winnie said with an admiring upward glance. "Somebody tell me to leave."

No one did.

"You're both too good, too polite," she said and left on her own.

Chief Jenkins climbed out of the Ford, regarded the roses, and remembered the pride the dentist had taken in them. He knew Cora Dray was there, somewhere. He could not see her, but he sensed her. He almost wanted to turn back. "I'm here," she said, and he sought the gate through the bushes.

She stood in a dark dress and dark stockings and gave him a straight clear stare. They had known each other since elementary school, a grade apart. "Cora, I'm sorry."

"Why?" she asked, not hearing him. "Why did you let Wilbur Cox break it to me? Why didn't you?"

"I'm sorry." His face showed it. "I should have."

"His wife was a servant here."

The chief shifted his feet uneasily and tried to read her face. It was indecipherable. "We have the medical report. He was shot, Cora."

She raised a hand. A truck was passing, the noise barreling through the screen of roses. She frowned, while the chief waited. His hand wanted to soothe hers, but she was not one to be touched. Nor, perhaps, to be consoled. "Trucks shouldn't be allowed on this street."

"Cora, he was shot."

"I heard you. Don't repeat it." Her eyes were unflickering. "It may have been an accident."

"That doesn't seem to be the case."

There was a shiver of a breeze. "I don't want people coming to my house. No reporters." Her chin lifted. "I'm a private person."

The chief was silent. She was his senior by a year and acted his superior by several degrees. He looked toward the house, the gingerbread fixings. He had never been inside, no reason to till now.

She said, "I hope I don't have to repeat everything I've already told Wilbur Cox. Everybody knows Stephen went jogging at odd hours."

"I know that."

"And I went to sleep. Soundly. And I slept late. I always

40

do. I wish now I'd never woken up."

"Cora." The chief sought to be diplomatic. "A lieutenant from the state police will probably ask you about his acquaintances."

"What acquaintances?" Her voice was sharp. "I know what you're getting at. Women went for him. That wasn't his fault." Her breasts rose under the dark dress. "He never laid a finger on any of them. He had too much respect for me."

"You're not playing fair, Cora."

"No." Something throbbed in her face. "Not when it comes to my good name. And his."

"Don't you want to know who killed him?"

"It won't bring him back." Her expression changed subtly, and the chief ceased to be seen. "My life is half empty now. No, not quite. I still have Bud." A smile, or what passed for one, played on her lips.

"Cora." He kept his voice level. "Is Bud here?"

"Yes, he is. Sleeping. And I'm not going to wake him. You scared him last night."

"Unintentionally. Cora. Does he own a gun?"

"No. He's afraid of them. So am I. So was Stephen." Her eyes dropped to his belt. "So are you." Quite deliberately she tightened her face. "Are you accusing Bud?"

"No, Cora."

"You'd better not. I'd kill you."

The chief looked at her, jarred. He turned to leave. "Tell him to come see me. When he can."

Winnie Wallace made her way down the bluff; the path was makeshift, treacherous here and there, but she knew where to drop a foot and where, definitely, not to. When she neared the spray she kicked off her sandals and tossed aside the towel she'd slung around her neck. It was not an easy place to swim and was particularly uninviting with the tide heaving in. Waves hit her full force, surged into her and over her, lifting her and shoving her aside. She hurled a shoulder against one, challenged another, and plunged into the third.

Five minutes later she was back on the pebbles, vigorously toweling herself dry. She faced the ocean and did not see the man lurching down the bluff, a rough descent for anyone who did not know the tricks. She was unaware of his presence until he reached bottom, stumbling, as if he had exhausted his legs. Pebbles rattled. She turned around.

"I scraped my goddamned hand," Sergeant Wilbur Cox said. "I hollered to you. Didn't you hear?"

She tossed her head, wet curls dangling, and gave a quick tug at the bottom of her bathing suit. "Down here you don't hear anything up there." She dropped forward to slip on her sandals, and Sergeant Cox viewed her breasts, a feast. His interest was obvious, and she said, "Easy, Wilbur. To me, you're the kid that used to spread manure at the Robertshaw farm."

"Come on!" he said, his voice snapping above the crack of the waves and his eyes all at once hating her. "Someone wants to talk to you."

"Who?"

"Lieutenant Haas, State Police. Waiting for you at your house."

She stood fixedly. "I've news for you, Wilbur. The chief has already talked to me."

"That don't count." He'd been waiting for her to say that, evidenced in the instant satisfaction of his smile. "Did you hear me?" he said, and her blue eyes gave off a daring flash.

"If the lieutenant wants to talk to me, tell him to come down here."

"Don't play fucking games."

"I don't like your mouth, Wilbur."

"I guess you like the chief's better."

"You belong back on the farm," she said coldly and looped the towel around her neck. "Let's go."

"After you, Miss America. That way I get to look at your ass."

She spun sideways, pebbles kicking up, and breezed by him. A gull screeched. She was halfway up the bluff while he was still struggling at the bottom.

Chief Jenkins pulled up beside the pumps at Skelly's Mobil on Route One, and Skelly lumbered toward him in greasy coveralls, her hair clipped like a man's and her neck seal-like over her widow's hump. She stopped a few feet away, wiping her hands on a rag. One of her hands made two of the chief's. She was younger than people suspected, and she was strong. The chief had once seen her lift the rear wheels of an Oldsmobile 98 off the ground. Some men in town called her Moby Dick, claiming that when her clothes were off she was the White Whale. She had, as far as the chief knew, appeared only once on a Boar's Bluff beach, and the disturbance had been immediate. The chief pushed open the door of the Ford and said, "I've got a tire that could use air."

Her voice rolled at him. "I sell gas, not air."

"I could use gas, too."

"Fill it?"

"Fine. Mind if I use your phone?"

She *did* mind but said nothing. She unhooked the hose and, pulling at it, walked it as if it were a snake whose neck she might wring. Popping the gas cap on the Ford, she drove the nozzle home with a clank. The chief entered the station through the garage, where an old car hovered on a lift and an even older one squatted over a grease pit. Though Skelly's heavy fingers seemed capable of nothing delicate, she was a master mechanic.

He phoned Sergeant Cox's house, and a girl answered with a deceivingly mature voice. The mind's eye of the chief saw a bit of a thing, but she doubtless was bigger now, perhaps nine years old, no more than ten. The chief asked for her mother and was told that she was not in.

"Do you know where she is?"

"Shopping. Who is this, please?"

"Do you know when she'll be back?"

"No. Who is this?"

The chief heard other children in the background. Gladys Cox had five altogether, closely spaced in ages, and the one on the line was the oldest. "It's nobody important," the chief said. "Tell her I'll call back."

Skelly waited for him at the pumps. "Only took two dollars," she said, a wide part of her face quivering with suspicion as her squeezed-in eyes drew upon him. "You didn't come here for gas. What did you come for?"

The chief's smile was not meant as mockery, but that was the way she took it. "Your phone," he said.

"Wasn't that either." The narrow intensity of her gaze was striking. Squaring herself, she emphasized the protective hulk of her body. "Is it about the dentist?"

The chief shrugged. "If there's anything you want to tell me, I'll listen."

"Maybe you want to arrest me."

"Why would I want to do that?"

"Because you don't know what you're doing."

"You're wrong, Skelly." The chief, who seemed to have fallen asleep on his feet, came alive. "If I was going to arrest you, I'd call in help from Hampton and Seabrook, and we'd all have guns."

★ ★ ★ ★ ★

Stephen Dray had practiced dentistry not in Boar's Bluff but in Hampton, in an office above a drugstore. The chief obtained a key from the druggist and browsed the dentist's files. Few patients were from Boar's Bluff. Many were from Hampton; more were from the lesser communities of Seabrook and Salisbury.

The druggist appeared, an old man, quite tiny, like a doll. The Aran cardigan he wore against the downstairs chill of the air-conditioner looked like a full-length coat on him. "Thought you might like this," he said, extending a Styrofoam cup of coffee. The chief accepted it gratefully, and the druggist said, "If you want to ask me anything, go ahead."

"I was wondering whether any patients were particularly friendly or unfriendly with Doctor Dray."

"I know what you're getting at." The druggist's smile was wry as he buried his baby hands into wide pockets. "But he cut that stuff out after the stink."

"What stink?"

"A few years ago, maybe four, he gave a female patient gas and then fooled around. You know, put his hands on her person, except she woke up before she should've and found her drawers around her knees. Her husband wanted to bring in the police, but I guess the dentist settled. They were Seabrook people, haven't been back since. I told all this to the state detective. He didn't seem too interested."

The chief wasn't either. "Did he have a secretary, dental assistant, someone like that?"

"No one he ever kept long. He was cheap about paying, and he closed the office every summer, you know, July first through Labor Day."

The chief tasted his coffee, which could have been hotter. In certain lights sadness seemed an intricate part of his face—

45

sadness over little things and big things.

The druggist said, "He wasn't a friend of yours, was he?"

"Everybody's my friend," the chief said and dropped his head back as though to nap. After the druggist stole away, he dumped the coffee into the spit bowl.

Daylight was fading when he pulled into his drive and saw the white Corvette glinting under the pines. He parked beside it and for a few moments sat immobile behind the wheel to listen to the giant guitar noise of a frog from a swampy section of the woods. Bud Brown stood on the far side of the Corvette, as if he had just planted himself there. Perhaps he had relieved himself behind a tree. The chief climbed out of the Ford and said, "Talk to me, Bud."

"What do you mean?" A breeze lifted the younger man's thin hair and revealed his baldness. "Talk to you about what?"

"Tell me things."

"What things?"

"I'll let you decide." The chief spoke from across the Corvette's hood, on which pine needles had fallen. There were a certain few ways to handle Bud Brown, and the chief was aware that he knew none of them and that maybe nobody did, except Cora Dray. "Take your time."

"Still don't know what you mean."

The chief brushed needles from the hood. "I like your car, Bud. I remember the day you got it from Skelly's Mobil. I was surprised the dentist sprang for it . . . until I realized there had to be a reason. This was when he was sweet on the minister's wife, and I figured you must've been looking through her window and saw something. And later I guess your sister must've said, 'Don't tell him you told me. Get something out of him.' Cora's mind goes that way."

Bud Brown's lips were silently drawn in. He brushed at a

mosquito. His hand was plump. He existed on snacks and milk shakes. "She said you wanted to see me."

"Her mind runs one way, yours another. I don't understand you, Bud. I wish I did." The chief sighed. "How many times have I got you out of scrapes? Have you kept count?"

He was open-mouthed for a moment, as though he might speak. But he didn't. The chief watched him closely.

"I'm scaring you, aren't I? I don't mean to. But I sometimes think you're smarter than you let on. Are you?"

Bud Brown looked through the pines to the road, where cars were passing, speeding, his excuse to stay silent. He was pale and subdued, and the breeze was bothering his hair again. His scalp was not pink but egg-white.

The chief said, "If you had to make a wild guess, Bud, who would you say killed him?"

The underlip quivered. "I don't know."

"I don't either," the chief said with the faintest of smiles. "That's why I was hoping you'd tell me."

He smeared mustard on bread and made a sandwich with a mixture of meat: bologna, boiled ham, salami. The owl hooted as he ate, and the telephone rang when he finished. The caller was Winnie Wallace, a commotion in her voice. "I've been trying to reach you," she said. "They grilled me."

"You knew they would."

"Haas his name is. Wilbur was with him."

"Yes, of course." The chief wiped his mouth. "Wilbur would've wanted to be in on it."

"Why the hell does he hate me?"

"Wilbur's peculiar that way."

"They told me they know more than I think." Notes of anger and panic were in her words. "What does that mean?"

"What did they say it meant?"

47

"They didn't say. They asked if I'd take a lie-detector test. I told them to go to hell."

The chief experienced a strange neutrality of feeling, which he knew would not last. "You're within your rights. But why don't you want to take one?" he asked and heard her pull in her breath.

"I couldn't bear being strapped up, all those gadgets attached to me. You know how I am. I won't even have my blood pressure taken." Her voice became small. "Paul, I'm afraid."

"You don't need to be." He carried the phone to the sink and turned on the tap.

"What are you doing?"

"Getting a drink of water." He let the water run. He wanted it as cold as he could get it. The radio was on in the bedroom, and he could hear Tony Bennett singing *Because of You*, which reminded him of Fort Devens. And he, the chief, a private, had been eighteen years old.

"Paul." Her tugging voice sounded as young as he was remembering himself. "Maybe I should have an alibi."

He drank his water, not as cold as he'd have liked it. "Why?" he asked. "Why do you need one?"

"Because I don't want the hassle, the scandal. It'd be bad for business. And Paul, I'm just plain scared."

"I'm on your side."

"Then be my alibi." She waited. She said, "I mean, if it comes to that."

"Let me think about it."

The Mobil station was closed. Skelly was in a curtained cubicle in the depths of the garage. The cubicle contained a metal cot and a chair, a sink and a shower stall, and a Sony television that was tuned to Johnny Carson. When a guest comedian recited an off-color joke, Skelly let out a belly laugh in anticipation of the punch line. Her head bobbed, and the cot shimmied.

She sat on the cot with her back against the rough wall and with her bare feet propped on the chair. She was naked under clean coveralls that, nevertheless, smacked of gasoline. Her body smelled of harsh soap, the gritty kind that came from a can. Dropping her feet to the floor, she leaned forward on the cot. Her ears were keen, and through the blare of a toothpaste commercial she heard a sound from the side of the station where a door had been left unlocked.

A tire iron lay beneath the cot. She did not reach for it. It was enough that she knew it was there. She waited, listening with a strained ear until she recognized the step. Then her mouth hardened into a near-smile.

"I knew you'd come," she said when a face appeared tentatively at the curtain's edge. She gave a swipe to her boy-like hair and turned the television down. "You been bad, Bud?"

"Don't worry about me," Bud Brown said, showing more of himself. He was sucking on something and sweating. His shirt showed several areas of damp. "*Quincy*'s on."

"I don't watch it. What are you eating?"

He reached into a pocket and produced disks of chocolate wrapped in gold paper to resemble coins. He plugged one into her hand and sat in the chair. She gave him a look.

"What are you sitting there for?"

He shrugged, his eye on the muted television. Johnny Carson was interviewing a starlet. A close-up showed her with her little finger in her mouth.

"You broke?"

He shook his head.

She unwrapped the candy and ate it while rolling the gold paper into a hard nugget. She grinned, showing tiny teeth.

"Then come here, for Christ's sake." When he was slow to move, she snapped the nugget at him.

A half-hour later, when Johnny Carson was signing off with a swing of an invisible golf club, headlights flared into the garage and lit the curtain. "Relax," Skelly said, a cigarette sloping from her mouth. "It's just somebody turning around." Her coveralls were heaped on the floor. She lay on the cot with her massive thighs still open. Suddenly she heaved herself up and gripped his wrist.

"You don't ever have to apologize to anybody, not even your sister." Had she chosen to, she could have crushed the wrist. "You're a man."

She freed him and dropped back to the cot, which wheezed under her weight.

"Got any more of those?"

"What?"

"The candies."

Six

The sun burnt away the early-morning mist, and the day turned hotter than the previous two. At times the sun seemed fierce enough to kindle the ocean, though it was only ten o'clock. Joan Weiss had been on the beach since seven, first to help Hetty Nelson gather shells and later to slouch in a chaise lounge as the beach crowded up. Eventually she tucked her book aside and torpidly pulled herself to her feet. Her face, deeply tanned, a copper case, gleamed out of a rich mass of brown hair. She was big-boned and thick-thighed, not tall enough to be statuesque but more than attractive enough to draw long looks, which she did not invite. She headed toward the surf, the heat of the sand livening her step.

The water swelled above her waist, and a cold current stung her legs. Pulling back a few steps, she used her hands to wet her face. When a jet from Pease passed over, she barely noticed it. Nor, for a long moment, did she notice that someone had waded near her and was standing slightly to her left. It was a man in sunglasses and magenta trunks.

"Too cold for you?" he asked, his smile like a crack in a saucer. Not knowing him, she regarded him indifferently. He said, "There are two more of you, aren't there?"

She started to glance away, and he laughed. She gave him a closer look. His hair, cut to caress his ears, was boyishly brushed across his forehead. He appeared to be a young fifty, with a pleasant face except for his mouth, which was violent when it laughed. He said, "You're from the gray house, aren't you?"

She nodded.

"I'm glad you three got it. Last year it was rented to Canadians with kids." His trunks were dry. The water swelled and stained the front of them as he moved closer to her. "A great house. I know the agent who leased it to you. In fact, I know her very well. I was married to her once." He expected a reaction and was disappointed. He stuck out a hand. The nails were polished. "Lyman Arnold."

"Weiss. Joan Weiss." She allowed a brief handshake, which he tried to prolong, smiling as he failed.

"Jewish, right?"

She looked askance at him. "As a matter of fact."

"Nice to know you. Until maybe twenty years ago no Jew stepped foot on a beach here."

"Yes," she said distantly, "I've heard the story."

He hovered. His chest was broad and hairless except for stray hairs around the nipples. He said, "The town's changed a lot since I was a kid. Now there are no safe places to swim naked."

"But of course you're no longer a kid."

"Touché." His smile was constant. "Did you hear the shot?"

"What shot?"

"The one that killed the dentist."

She flinched. "No."

"Apparently nobody did. Wasn't loud enough, I guess." The ocean air shuddered around them. A squall of children stormed by, much splashing. "You scared?"

"Uncomfortable. We knew the man slightly."

"What did you think of him?"

She did not wish to answer, but she did. "I can't say we liked him."

"I know what you mean." He pulled at his trunks, his belly nipped in. His smile turned subtle. "You have a married look. Are you?"

Again she did not wish to answer. The conversation had quickly become predictable. The water pushed against them, swelling between them and soaking his trunks. The tide was coming in, each wave a blade. "No," she said, "I'm not married."

"But you have been," he guessed, and his eyes consumed her. "I like your other bathing suit better. The pink one." The long cut of his mouth became a grin. "Yes, I've seen you in it. It shows more of you."

She'd had enough. She tried to move past him, back to the shore. He was in the way. An unbroken wave pushed them together for an instant, and she felt his breath vibrate against her cheek.

"Shall we take a quick swim?"

"No," she said, seaweed floating between her ankles. "This is as far as I go." She got by him. He called after her.

"By the way, thanks for the invitation."

She half turned, staring hard. "What are you talking about?"

"You're having a party, aren't you? You invited the Smiths, fifth cottage up. They're friends of mine. You told them to bring along anyone they liked, and they're bringing me."

Her smile, slow to appear, was neutral.

"What's the matter? Afraid I might be the murderer?"

"You could be, I suppose, but I rather doubt it."

He laughed. "I should warn you. I've known a couple of Jewish women named Joan."

She held back her response, afraid it would be too cutting, and waded away.

★ ★ ★ ★ ★

Sergeant Wilbur Cox ate breakfast in the dining room of the Coral Motel, two miles from Philpott's, on the boulevard. He had dripped a bit of syrup on his chin, where it had dried like shellac. Lieutenant Haas sat across from him. The lieutenant, a fastidious eater, dug a spoon into a baked peach half and said, "I didn't realize the civilian was his mother-in-law."

"Sure. A lot of us don't like it. She never took an exam or nothing."

"When did his wife die?"

"Years ago. They weren't married more than a couple of years. She had something in her brain that went, all of a sudden. The joke is she died in another guy's arms."

"Is that true?"

"I'm just repeating the joke. I guess it was on a dance floor."

The lieutenant smeared jelly over toast. His bite was small. "When did Winnie Wallace pop into his life?"

"Hell, he's always known her. Before and after his marriage, maybe even *during* for all I know." Sergeant Cox pushed his plate aside. The waitress refilled his coffee cup. "Thanks, honey."

"Wipe your chin," Lieutenant Haas said.

"What?"

"You have something on it."

The sergeant knotted a napkin and rubbed hard. "Her marriage didn't last long either, you know. It was annulled. The guy's family didn't like her. They had money."

"Did she get any of it?"

"They settled something on her, that's for sure."

"That's a nice house she lives in."

"That belonged to her parents. They're dead. The house

54

was never much to look at until she put a pile of money into it."

The lieutenant did not finish his toast, not caring for the jelly, which was apricot. His pinched nostrils sighed open. "How does she do in her real estate business?"

"She's a hustler. Works for less commission than the other brokers, which is why they don't like her. I mean, she was doing that even before mortgage rates went up."

"It's a cutthroat business."

"She's perfect for it." Sergeant Cox leaned over his coffee with an extreme air of confidentiality. "She still our candidate?"

"She intrigues me," Lieutenant Haas said, gazing through the wide window at guests of the motel, early birds on the beach. "She's an interesting creature."

"I read body English," Sergeant Cox said. "I'm good at it. Hers tells me she'd cut a guy's balls off without thinking about it. My opinion is that after the dentist dumped her she went ape."

Lieutenant Haas did not comment, perhaps did not hear.

"And you really shook her up when you mentioned the polygraph."

Lieutenant Haas used a napkin on his fingers. "She intrigues me, and so does your chief. I don't know whether he's stupid or shrewd."

"Want my opinion?"

"I think I know it."

The sergeant lifted his coffee cup without using the handle. "It's tough working for him. He don't even come close to being a good cop."

Lieutenant Haas continued to gaze at the boiling beach with its glaring surfaces and simmering levels of flesh.

The sergeant said, "They never should've made him chief.

Do you want to know which selectman pushed the appointment? It's ironic."

Lieutenant Haas motioned for the check. "I'm listening."

Sergeant Cox grinned. "The guy his wife was dancing with when she died. Ed Robertshaw."

The house was a yellow frame on a treeless lot on the slope of a back road. Plastic toys littered the parched front lawn. A rusting tricycle lay broken. Chief Jenkins rapped on the side door and called through the screen. The somber face of a girl nine or ten scrutinized him. "Hi, sweetheart, your mother in?" he asked, and she opened the door. The kitchen was taken up by a homemade bar. Younger children peered at him from behind boxes of sugary breakfast cereal.

"She's doing a wash," the girl said in a voice that made her seem twice her age. The chief could hear the rumble beneath his feet, the banging of water pipes.

"That the door?"

He descended narrow stairs, dimly illuminated. Beyond a doorless opening, he saw a carpeted space containing a small made-up bed. Straight ahead was the gloom of the laundry room.

"Gladys," he called out in warning. "Paul Jenkins."

Gladys Cox did not hear him. She was bent over dirty clothes, heaps of them, her movements mechanical as she sorted colors. She was blondish and short, vaguely pretty but chunky. Her housedress was soaked under the arms. The chief forced his voice above the action of the washer.

"Gladys."

She jumped.

"Sorry," he said, stepping around a pile of underclothes, her children's and some of her own. All seemed frayed. She viewed him with dull unreflective eyes. Her eyebrows were faint, her mouth turned down at the corners.

"What do you want?" she said tonelessly. He had to strain to hear her.

"I phoned yesterday."

"Was that you? Laurie told me someone called."

"I can't hear you."

They moved partway out of the laundry room, she reluctantly. Her eyes were downcast, and her fingers reeked of bleach. The chief could see into the room with the bed.

"Who sleeps there?"

"It's extra, that's all."

"You do sometimes, right?" His eyes were doleful. "Does Wilbur still belt you around?"

"I can handle him."

"I could speak to him."

"You did that once before. It didn't help."

The chief paused to deliberate. "Gladys. I'm going to tell you something and then ask a couple of questions. It's important that you answer truthfully."

"Why shouldn't I?"

"As you probably know, Wilbur is working closely with Lieutenant Haas of the State Police in the Dray death. He's given Haas a list of women the dentist was friendly with. Past and present."

Her eyes slid away from his, and her face went white. He could tell she was holding her breath.

"Gladys," he said with all the sympathy of a much older brother, "it's okay. Your name isn't on it."

Her relief was immediate and revealing. She tried to recover. "What are you talking about? Are you trying to insult me?"

"Gladys, don't. Don't pretend. I'm not here to hurt you, but I've got to have the truth. Do you understand? Gladys, please look at me." He spoke slowly. "Do you understand?"

She drew the unattended hair from her face and nodded.

"Did Wilbur know or ever suspect?"

She shook her head.

"Are you sure?"

Her laugh was bitter. "I wouldn't be alive, would I?" She breathed deeply. "Why do you want to know about Wilbur?"

"I thought he might be protecting you . . . or more likely himself."

She dropped her voice and spoke from pale lips. "Now can I ask you something? How did you know about me and . . . Doctor Dray?"

"I once saw you talking to him in Philpott's. I caught a glimpse of your face."

She closed her eyes for a moment. "I'd been doing housework for his wife, and she fired me. She knew. Do you know what she said to me? She said she could smell him on me. That became his excuse to break it off. Actually he was already seeing somebody else. It was your whore, Paul. Winnie Wallace."

The chief winced. "She's not a whore, anymore than you are."

"You don't know what I am. Nobody does." Her face was suddenly and vividly flushed. It blazed over the aggressive thrust of her chin. The chief started to turn away; she touched him high on the sleeve, giving him a sweeping whiff of bleach. "He treated me nice for a while. It wasn't the sex that mattered. I didn't even want any."

"You don't have to explain."

"He had to jimmy my knees open the first time. Maybe that's what made me exciting to him. For a while. Nothing good lasts long, does it?" Her face constricted as she drew back into herself. Her hand fell from his sleeve. "So you're not going to ask if I did it?"

He shrugged. "Should I?"

"If you were Wilbur, you could beat a confession out of me."

The chief moved toward the stairs and saw the girl, Laurie, at the top. The woman the child would too soon be peered somberly down at him. He shrank back and murmured, "I think she heard us."

"I trust her." Gladys Cox's face was a shadow beneath her hair, and her laugh was low and unhappy. "She's the only one I do."

By mid-afternoon the beach had emptied somewhat. Waves snapped at the sand. Laura Kimball, smelling harshly of the ocean, toweled herself, slipped a chambray shirt over her bathing top, and smiled down at the baked and burnished figure of Joan Weiss. "How can you take so much sun?"

Joan looked up from her bent-back chair, white nails glistening from the brown hand shading her eyes. Her wheat-colored hair was laced with lighter strands. "My mother couldn't get enough of it. When it got too cold to sit out, she stayed by a window on the sun side of the house."

Laura hunkered beside the chair. "You mean, toward the end."

"Yes. Knowing you're going to die, she said, was like standing out in the cold. You couldn't forget for a second how cold you were. It was always pulling at you, she said, letting you know you could never get warm."

"Do you realize," Laura said, "this is the first time you've said more than two words about it? At least to me."

Joan gave out a dim smile. "My mother didn't acknowledge the disease at first. The initial sweetness of it was too serious to discuss, too surreal even to allude to. The day she told my father he walked out the door and never came back."

"The bastard," Laura said, the epithet more a lip movement than a sound.

"No. Not really. He was simply a weak character. He couldn't bear to watch her die."

"He left that to you."

Both women went silent. Laura spread her towel and sat on it, embracing a raised knee and staring off. Eddies of children swirled at the water's edge, with a mother or two looking after them. Joan, sitting erect, straightened the back of her chair. Then she pointed to the surf, beyond where Laura was gazing. "Isn't that Pam? Way out."

Laura cast her eye in that direction and glimpsed a head in the water, beyond the waves. "I wish she wouldn't go out so far."

"She's a good swimmer."

They watched Pamela Comeau swim parallel with the beach. Her stroke was swift, as if she were trying to tire herself out. Her blond hair, soaked against her skull, glowed. Of the three women, Pamela usually seemed the most prudent and steady, possibly because she was skilled at diminishing outward signs of tension through physical activity. When her marriage was reduced to a legal waltz between lawyers, she took up tennis, and later, after the divorce, when someone named Roger devastated her, she took up the game again. Now, with other problems pressing on her, she was turning herself into a strong swimmer.

Joan said, "Good, she's coming in."

They watched her coast in with a wave that seemed to spread wide for her. A gull glided toward her and abruptly peeled to the right. They watched her mingle with children and talk with a mother.

"Did she get through to Seattle?" Joan asked.

"I don't think so. She'd have said something." Laura smoothed back her dark hair, her brow knotting. "I don't see why they can't at least return her calls."

"Where's it written that kids have to care?"

"In the womb," Laura said, looking away. She heard the creak of a man struggling to his feet to go to the water. Then she peered past him, far to her left. "There's our friend."

The bent and bonneted figure of Hetty Nelson was near the boulders where the body of the dentist had lain. The old woman spat on the spot, which seemed sinister, heavy with motive, but she was merely clearing her throat.

Joan said quietly, "She's coming to the party tonight. She invited herself."

"I'm getting bad vibes. Not about her. About the party. I wish we knew the people better." Laura hugged her knee harder.

"I know. Do you want to cancel?"

"I'm not sure. Pam's already made the punch. That might send people home early."

"Let's flip. Odds we cancel."

"I don't have a coin."

"Do fingers."

Laura thrust out three. So did Joan.

Pamela approached, a slender figure in white. She had snatched up her sleeveless robe along the way and was wearing it. "What are you two doing?"

Joan said, "I wish we knew."

Chief Jenkins spoke his piece. Lieutenant Haas viewed him from a different perspective than before and said soberly, "Do you know what you're doing?"

They were in the chief's office, the door closed. Sergeant

Cox was present but ignored. The sergeant wanted to speak but did not quite dare. A mosquito whined near his ear, and he gave his head a violent shake.

"Are you prepared to call me a liar?" the chief asked.

"Almost," Lieutenant Haas said. His nose prickled. "Why'd you wait?"

"I never thought Miss Wallace would become a serious suspect."

"I don't buy that."

Sergeant Cox found courage. "What makes it look bad, Chief, is that she stayed the night with you. Makes it look like—what do you call it?—a meringue a twat."

The chief ignored him, while Lieutenant Haas repressed a smile. The chief turned red. Strengthening the timbre of his voice, he said, "She's not as tough as she acts. If you keep coming down on her she'll go to pieces. And you still won't have your killer."

Sergeant Cox wanted to speak again, but something told him to stay silent. The mosquito migrated to the ear of the chief, who endured the bite. Lieutenant Haas gave him an oblique glance.

"She didn't kill him, who did?"

"He might've done it himself. There were powder burns."

"The gun, Chief. Did he throw it in the ocean afterwards?"

"Somebody might've walked away with it. A kid could've."

"Doesn't ring right. In fact, it doesn't ring at all." The lieutenant rose. "You change your attitude on this, give me a call. I live in Exeter. Your sergeant's got my number."

He left.

The chief scratched at his ear, drawing blood. Sergeant Cox, sitting squarely, immobile, said, "You don't really be-

62

lieve he popped himself, do you? I mean, a load of shit like that is insulting to the lieutenant."

The chief stared at Sergeant Cox's breast pocket, at the silver glint in the top corner.

"I think you made a mistake, Chief. You might have even cut your throat."

"Is that my pen, Wilbur?"

"Yeah, Chief." Sergeant Cox returned it with a flourish. "You might need it to write your resignation."

Seven

It was not expected to be an overly large party, but it began to grow. The guests were mostly from the cottages, a few from the larger dwellings beyond, and all had a guest or two of their own. Some women were dressed casually, others to the nines. A number of men wore voile shirts through which chest hair and nipples could be seen. Lyman Arnold, however, wore a blue flannel blazer and challis tie. He pushed his way to the drinks table with the Smiths. Mr. Smith wore a turtleneck jersey that crested his chin, and Mrs. Smith had on Calvin Klein jeans. Her lip paint gave her a peach smile and a false air of youth. The drinks table disappointed her. It offered only punch, beer, and wine, nothing hard. Lyman Arnold slung a commiserating arm around her.

Mr. Smith popped open a can of Michelob. "I can't keep the hostesses straight."

"It's easy." Mrs. Smith lit a Virginia Slim. "The tall thing with the endless legs is Laura, the stunning blonde is Pat—or is it Pam?—and the husky handsome one is Jane."

"Joan," Lyman Arnold said.

Mrs. Smith stood corrected. "Who's your favorite, Lyman?"

"I don't know yet."

"Which one's vulnerable?" she asked with a note of sarcasm. He poured punch. It was for her. People gathered behind them.

"I haven't figured that out yet," he said.

64

"But you will," she said, disdaining the punch. "I want wine."

Her husband, handing her a full glass, had anticipated her preference but not the color. "I want white," she said.

She carried it away with her, into the crowd, into the unexpected company of a neighbor, a chiropractor with a practice in Concord. Blond and big, like a buccaneer, he was one of those wearing a voile shirt, but with a jacket over it. Her eyes asked him something, and they edged from one room to another into a private place. He reached into his jacket. "It's not Acapulco Gold," he said, "but it'll do."

"You're a lifesaver," she said.

Joan, conferring with the caterer, detected the scent. She knew it well. Her son's room used to reek of it. As quickly as possible, she finished her conversation with the caterer and raised a window shade to let in air. Moisture from the sea dribbled in. She looked down to find Hetty Nelson at her side. For the party, the old woman had somehow stained and burnt her sparse hair into scarlet ringlets, which looked like afflictions on her scalp, and she had pasted color to her lips in an effort to enlarge them. Her odd-hanging dress smelled of mothballs and made her look like a rag doll.

"I had some of that punch. I hope it doesn't make me sick."

"There's not much alcohol in it," Joan said, but the old woman was not listening. Her tiny head was tipped toward the screen in the window so that she could better hear the distant rumble of waves, which never failed to revive memories.

"I lost my little brother out there. A fisherman found him three days later off Seabrook. That was seventy years ago. Now it's like it never happened."

"Hetty, I'm sorry. I didn't know."

"I helped stack sandbags on the beach, I forget which war,

first or second. Maybe both. And I used to look for U-boats through a spyglass. People don't remember."

Joan touched the old woman's shoulder, nothing but bone.

"I know secrets that would scare people. But nobody has to worry. I never tell tales."

"I'm sure you don't."

Hetty Nelson peered up with salty eyes through a crust of makeup. "I don't take to a lot of people," she said and abruptly gripped the younger woman's hand. "But I like you."

Heavy footsteps passed behind them. Voices shot up from another room, where furniture had been pushed against the walls to make more space. The laughter of women was loudest. Men shouted to be heard.

"My head hurts," Hetty Nelson said. "Do you mind if I leave early?"

"Of course not."

"After I eat."

Chief Jenkins parked the Ford near the gray house but did not get out. He listened to the reverberation of voices and the occasional bursts of laughter and tried to glimpse Winnie Wallace's silhouette among the many darkening the lighted windows. She had wanted him to take her to the party, and he had said he might join her later. Now he was at odds with himself, wanting neither to join her nor to disappoint her. He had not been to a party since his wife had died at one. He slipped out of the Ford.

Skirting the rays of light from the gray house, he let the fierce surge of the night sweep him onto the beach. Only a bit of moon showed. Soft-footedly he followed the surf from one empty bathing area to another. Hearing young voices, he avoided them, though they seemed quite distant and thoroughly disembodied. He stopped and sat on dry sand, letting the darkness consume him. A dull rage built as he allowed himself to dwell on raw events in his life. Sitting back, half lying on his elbows, he remembered the immediate years after his wife's death and how he had accepted the loss a little more each day as the house gradually shed her traces. His things, his solitary ways, took over each room. If she was anywhere now, she was inside him when he least expected her.

A girl's shriek lifted him off his elbows. A boy's bark followed the shriek, kids cutting up, beer bottles tinkling. Feet pounded on hard sand, far enough away to ignore. Slowly he sank back on his elbows. It was, at times, pleasant for him to succumb to loneliness, the way that he sometimes enjoyed the ache in his bad leg. He stretched the leg. When he again heard the shriek, he knew it came from Charlene Farnham.

She did not sound drunk, and he did not move.

Pamela Comeau replenished the punch bowl. As she squeezed away from the table, a bespectacled woman from one of the larger summerhouses brushed her arm and said, "Do sit with me and talk." They weaved toward chairs just vacated. The woman, wearing a short dress that gave out a violet glow, was birdlike and fidgety, with a pointed mouth breaking off into sharp smiles. Even seated, she seemed in motion, her gaudy glasses reflecting splinters of light. "A wonderful idea, the party. It gives us all a chance to talk about the dentist. Did you know him well?"

Pamela smiled at faces cutting across her line of vision. She heard a piercing laugh. "No, not well. Though we often saw him on the beach."

"Such a silly man. Always showing off his bump. I'm sure he thought he was Charles Atlas." The woman had wine with her. She sipped quickly. "A tragedy, though. An act of passion, my husband says. He thinks a woman did him in. I think it was a jealous husband."

"Have you tried the punch?"

"Yes, dear. I'll stick with this." The woman quickened her voice. "Of course, the wife is a real bird. Along with the brother. Hers. I suppose in Boston murder's taken for granted. There's so much of it, I mean, and you seldom know the people. Here, of course, it's an event."

Pamela, feeling claustrophobic, waited for a nearby swell of voices to subside. She had the impression that the speakers were trying to out-babble each other before returning to the buffet table for seconds. She said, "Have you eaten?"

"Yes, dear. Probably too much. You girls put out a nice spread."

"Would you excuse me?"

The woman's smile faded. "Of course, dear."

Pamela pressed through the crowd, here and there greeting those she hadn't met yet or greeting again those she'd failed to remember. Near the pantry two lean men were arguing and appeared ready to go at it, bone to bone. Then she realized they were only playing around, jibing each other. "Wonderful party," another man said, joggling near as if to give her a tickle under the arm. Later, near the stairs, she spoke briefly with Laura Kimball.

"Is it a disaster?"

"No," Laura whispered. "Just not what we intended."

Pamela started to climb the stairs to fetch aspirin but stopped when voices filtered down and shadows bent her way. She retreated.

"Please," Chief Jenkins said. "Don't be afraid." He was a dark figure near the surf, and Joan Weiss stopped short when she saw him. She had walked Hetty Nelson home and was taking a round-about way back to the gray house. The chief said, "I didn't mean to frighten you."

She made out his face in the scant moonlight. Behind him a bed of pebbles rang out each time a wave remade it. "Who are you?"

"Paul Jenkins."

The name meant nothing to her, but the face was familiar and the voice reassuring. "I've seen you on the beach before, haven't I? Not in a bathing suit. I'd have remembered." She put a hand to her mouth and almost laughed. "My God, I didn't mean that the way it sounded. What I mean is that when people are in bathing suits, all the good and bad shows."

"You're missing your party."

"Yes, I know. But how did you know?" The gray house was many fragments of light in the distance. She waited for him to answer.

"I like to know who my summer people are."

With a flash of inspiration, she said, "You're the police chief."

He shifted his stance, favoring a leg. "Aren't you afraid to be on the beach at night after what happened?"

"You can't live your life being afraid. In Cambridge I have triple locks on my door. I didn't think I'd have to do it here."

"You never know."

"Yes, that's already been proved."

"Did you know the dentist?"

"People keep asking me that. Not well. Not well at all."

"Then you didn't form an opinion of him?"

"Yes, I did, Chief. But do you mind if I keep it to myself?"

"I probably know it."

"You probably do."

They began tramping away from the surf and in the general direction of the gray house. The darkness was a swirl. She turned at his touch, his hand a surprise on her arm. At the same time she heard moans and sighs up ahead. "We'd better avoid that," he said.

"Kids?"

"Great to be young."

"Whatever happened to holding hands?"

"You tell me."

"Are we old-fashioned, Chief?"

"I think so."

More moon was visible by the time they neared the lighted gray house, which looked aluminized. Windows were milk-white. Voices were loud. "You're welcome to come in," she said. "There might even be some food left."

He declined. "Thanks just the same."

"By the way," she said, extending a hand, "I'm Joan Weiss."

"I know."

"I see. It's your business to know."

"Yes." He held her hand longer than necessary and released it reluctantly.

There was too much cigarette smoke. It made Pamela Comeau's eyes water. In desperate need of cool air, she slipped out onto the porch, progressed slowly along the rail, and paused under the hanging fuchsia. But not for long. She was near a window and did not want to overhear conversation. She advanced farther along, past more windows, where moths quivered against the screens. It was not until she followed the porch to another side of the house, into the shadows, that she sensed that somebody was softly dogging her steps. A voice said, "You're the one that wears the robe. No sleeves."

She spun around.

A pampered fifty-year-old face narrowed its eyes on her. Then the man edged closer, and she smelled what he had been drinking, nothing from the house, something he must have brought with him. "I wish you had it on now. I love you in it."

She did not know him, though his carefully styled hair seemed familiar. Doubtless she had greeted him earlier, but she could not dredge up a name.

"I've been watching you all evening."

There was a sudden terrible edge on her nerves as she tried to compute ways to breeze by him with no scene, no ugliness. His eyes grew more intimate.

"I bet you're the best. Of the three, I mean."

She started to push past him, but he thrust a shoulder in the way. "Please, I don't need this," she said coldly, which appeared to amuse him.

"The three of you summering here alone, tell me you're not looking for action," he challenged and was ready to put hands on her when a footfall startled him and then a voice.

"She's not interested, Lyman, can't you see?" Winnie Wallace, boldly displayed in a sheath dress, smiled through a fiery shade of lipstick. As she took a full breath she seemed to grow larger, her presence heavier, her décolletage more formidable. "She finds you disgusting. I do, too."

At first, his lips pinched, Lyman Arnold refused to look directly at her. Then he did so slowly. "You old bag," he said with utmost contempt.

Chief Jenkins was home. Sleep came fast, full of dreams. In one, his wife gave him a slowly diminishing smile. As her smile faded, so did she. Another dream put him back into the army. It seemed nothing would wake him, but something did. A touch, a voice perhaps, he wasn't sure. Winnie Wallace's face loomed spectrally. Her knee struck the bed. "Move over," she said with urgency and slipped under the covers without taking off her sheath, which smelled of sea air and brine and was damp all over, sopping at the hem.

"Where've you been?"

"Please, Paul," she said. "Let me sleep."

Eight

It was seven a.m. The imminence of rain filmed the sky and cooled the air. Chief Jenkins drove along Ocean Boulevard to a remote coastal point where Ed Robertshaw, the town's wealthiest man and the head of the oldest family, maintained an old fishing shack as a retreat from his three spinster sisters. His daughter, Amy, was married to Lyman Arnold. Robertshaw money, originally derived from a dairy farm and an apple orchard, now came chiefly from highway construction and real estate. As Wilbur Cox had once shoveled manure for Ed Robertshaw, Chief Jenkins had once picked apples.

The chief parked near the shack and walked over private sand to the ocean. The large raw head of a bald man bobbed in the water. The chief smiled and waved and then shivered as a damp breeze penetrated his shirt. The water was cold. Ed Robertshaw, his body bruised from the elements, waded in rubbing his genitals.

The chief glanced around. "No towel?"

Ed Robertshaw slapped himself dry. He was in his sixties and, despite a belly that overlapped his trunks, was more muscled than many men half his age. His blue-lipped smile revealed sturdy teeth. He said, "Great way to start off the day. Try it sometime."

"I'd collapse."

Ed Robertshaw ran his hands, large and stubby, over his bald head and glanced back at the ocean. "You know, a few minutes ago, just before you came, I could've sworn I saw a shark. About seventy-five yards out. You see anything?"

The chief shook his head. "Might have been a sand shark."

"The fin looked big. If it was a fin." They began tramping toward the shack, where gulls were perched on the roof. Ed Robertshaw gave the chief a sidelong glance. "You look puffy around the eyes. Rough night?"

"I didn't get much sleep."

"Your mother-in-law tell you I was trying to reach you?"

"Yes."

"She was pretty in her day."

"Alice?"

"Yes, she was."

They paused outside the shack, which from the outside gave the weather-beaten illusion that Ed Robertshaw was roughing it. Inside, the chief knew, were paneling and carpeting and modern conveniences, including an electric toilet.

"Want to come in for coffee?"

"I'm kind of pressed. The Dray case."

Ed Robertshaw was surprised. "You're not handling that yourself, are you? My understanding is the state police are."

"That's true." The chief stood with hands clasped behind his back. "Though, of course, I'm keeping myself informed."

"Naturally." Ed Robertshaw shook his shoulders to ward off a chill. "That's why I was trying to reach you. I want to stay informed myself, in case there's any scandal brewing for the town, not that murder isn't scandal enough."

The chief agreed with a look. Ed Robertshaw briskly rubbed one arm and then the other. He snapped at his trunks.

"I never did understand why Cora Brown married somebody like that. I thought she had sense. I knew her father. Have the state boys come up with anything?"

"Nothing concrete."

Ed Robertshaw squinted. "Could Cora have done it?"

"If she were going to kill her husband, she'd have done it years ago."

"What about her brother? No secret he's got a screw loose."

"Bud's a coward."

"I know you say he's harmless, but not everybody agrees. One of these days he's going to get his head blown off peeking in windows."

"I'm not sure he does it anymore."

Ed Robertshaw scratched at the salt drying in his chest hair. "One other thing. I got a message last night your sergeant was trying to reach me. What's his name?"

"Wilbur."

"That's him. The kid that used to shovel shit for me. What's he want?"

After a split-second hesitation the chief said, "No idea."

"He should go through channels. Doesn't he know that?"

"I'll tell him."

"Keep me informed, Paul."

"I will."

Lieutenant Haas conferred with the district attorney behind a closed door in the Exeter courthouse. The district attorney, known to his cronies as Chugger, a childhood nickname, was gaunt, gray-skinned, and tired-looking, with a history of heart attacks. He was a good listener, which allowed him to save his voice and conserve his strength. He listened as if writing everything down in his head. Finally he said, "What makes you so sure the police chief is lying?"

"He does it badly."

"Some people tell the truth unconvincingly. I've lost cases because of them."

"This is different."

"But so far you have no hard evidence against the Wallace woman. And you're working on a gut feeling about the chief."

"More or less," Lieutenant Haas said. "At this point I thought I might need a little guidance. I don't know whose toes I might crush."

The district attorney lit a forbidden cigarette. "Probably nobody's, but who knows." The district attorney coughed. "Stay with it. But keep me posted."

Lieutenant Haas nodded and left. The district attorney picked up his private telephone and put a call through to a ranking state Republican committeeman in Concord. "Charlie, this is Chugger," he said. "I have a potential situation that could be good for me or could be bad." Then he explained, smoothly and quickly, in short sentences.

"Hold on," the other man said. Nearly five minutes passed before he came back on the line. "Jenkins, you said, right? We don't seem to know much about him. He must be nonpolitical. However, he's on Ed Robertshaw turf. Do you know Ed?"

"Not personally."

"I'd advise you to check with him, a matter of courtesy. And of course, Chugger, keep me informed."

"Of course."

The telephone rang. Alice Cross picked it up and said, "Police. May I help you? . . . No, he's not in. What's the problem, Mrs. Myatt? . . . Well, you don't want the chief for that . . . Yes, Mrs. Myatt, I know about the leash law . . . Now calm down. I'll see what I can do."

She pushed her coffee mug to one side and raised Officer Leo Morin on the radio, along with much static, probably interference from Pease. She had to shout. "Where are you, Leo? . . . Have you seen anything of the chief? . . . What? . . .

Well, if you do see him, tell him to call me . . . Damn it, Leo, his radio doesn't work. If it did, I wouldn't be asking you, would I? . . . Be quiet and listen. I want you to go over to Lodge Road. The Farnham's dog chased Mrs. Myatt's cat up a tree, and it won't come down . . . Don't sass me, Leo. Just do what I say."

The chief stared down at her. "Morning," he said, and she gave a start.

"You're late again, and you look like hell," she said. He shrugged and turned away. His hair overlapped the back of his collar. "You need a haircut."

"You sound like a mother-in-law."

"That's what I am."

He headed toward his office. She wanted to leap up and seize him by the shoulders.

"Why?" she asked. "Why are you protecting Winnie Wallace?"

He looked back. "Some things aren't your business," he said in a voice as gentle as he could make it. The words hurt him as much as they did her.

"Thanks," she said. "Thanks for putting me in my place."

Hetty Nelson stood against a great smell of seaweed that was damp on the surface and thoroughly soaked underneath, some of it slammed against rocks. She had on a bonnet and a dress that hung unevenly, high in front, low in back. Water charged over her ankles, and her sneakered feet spaded into the drowned sand. Joan Weiss saw her from a distance and hurried toward her.

"Hetty, be careful."

The eyes were unsteady dots. "I'm looking for something. I found one body. Why shouldn't I find another?"

Joan staggered back, and Hetty Nelson smiled.

★ ★ ★ ★ ★

On the beach behind the Coral Motel the lifeguard sat with dangling legs atop an orange rig and chatted with girls peering up at him. Farther away a man roaming the sand with a metal detector, in search of money, edged the device toward a clump of washed-up rope. In time his attention was taken by a young woman and two children. The children were pot-bellied boys, pre-schoolers with shovels and pails. Their mother, proud of her schoolgirl shape, wore a bikini. As the boys dug sand, she waded into the surf up to her hips. She raised her arms, took a breath, and plunged into a wave.

She swam against the grain of the ocean, using a short and sharp stroke and a smooth kick.

She did not see the murky shape drifting toward her. It was more than half submerged, and it had eyes. When she barged into it, the silent mass reared up.

Her scream was muted, most of it locked in her throat.

On the beach her sons threw wet sand at each other, and the man with the device unearthed a nickel. The lifeguard re-arranged his legs in a way that the girls below could see the filled harness under his neon swim trunks. A stray cloud blotted some of the sun.

One of the boys pointed with his shovel. "Look at Mommy."

A minute later the lifeguard leaped off his rig, sprinted over the sand, and crashed into the surf. He pulled the hysterical woman to shore. The sea-ravaged corpse of Lyman Arnold washed in on its own.

Nine

It was ten in the evening. The town hall was dark except for the section housing the police station, which was ablaze. Chief Jenkins parked the Ford between two state vehicles. Television and newspaper reporters stood in a knot in the lighted lot, all of them drinking coffee from paper cups. They were preparing to leave. The chief, his shirt hanging loose over his chinos, received little notice. None seemed to know who he was.

He was not surprised to see Alice Cross still at her desk, though she should have left hours ago. The phones would not stop ringing. People were scared.

Her relief, Bess Cook, was also taking calls. "Paul," she spoke low so that Bess would not hear. "I'm sorry about this morning."

"My fault, not yours." He moved on to his office.

Lieutenant Haas had made himself home at the chief's desk, and two young troopers were in nearby chairs. Sergeant Wilbur Cox was in a distant chair, as if he'd been edged out. Lieutenant Haas introduced his detectives, Hector and Mack, and said to one, "Get the chief a chair."

"I'm okay." The chief shoved his hands into his pockets. He bristled over the invasion of his office and tried not to feel threatened by it. "Any developments?"

Lieutenant Haas tipped back in the chief's chair. "Still waiting to hear from the medical examiner. He's working overtime for us."

79

"So we still know nothing definite."

"I wouldn't say that." Lieutenant Haas let a few seconds pass. "We can presume the puncture in the stomach was from a gunshot. The interesting thing is the chunk torn out of the victim's thigh. Have you ever seen a shark-bite, Chief?"

"Only in *Jaws*."

The two troopers shuffled their feet, their eyes flicking over the chief. Lieutenant Haas's smile was formal and almost cold. He said, "My theory is that the victim, wounded and terrified, fled his assailant by running the best he could into the ocean, where he died of his wound or drowned or, perhaps, succumbed to the shock of a shark attack. A combination of things. Whichever way it comes out, it's homicide."

"What was he doing at the Coral Motel?" the chief asked.

"We don't think he was doing anything there. The Coast Guard says the body could've drifted, which fits with what we know. He was at a party last night, a house overlooking the same beach where the dentist was scratched. What do you think of coincidences, Chief?"

The chief said nothing.

Lieutenant Haas said, "I don't like them."

The chief felt the eyes of the two troopers glued to him. He shot a glance at Sergeant Cox, whose sour silence seemed imposed. The room was close. Too many people breathing in it.

"I understand," Lieutenant Haas said without inflection, "your friend was once married to Arnold."

"Years ago."

"And she was at the party last night."

"I believe so."

"You know so, don't you?"

The chief was stiff and still.

"Where was she afterward?"

"With me."

"Were you at the party?"

"No."

"Perhaps," Lieutenant Haas said, "we should speak privately."

"I don't see the need," the chief said.

All the same, the two troopers, Hector and Mack, heaved themselves out of their chairs. Sergeant Cox received a sign and rose with a jerk. "I think I'll have myself a coffee," he said. With a swagger he followed the two troopers out of the office, slapping the door shut behind him.

Lieutenant Haas said, "Sit down, Chief. You make me nervous."

"That's my desk."

"You want it?"

"No. I'm just reminding you."

The telephone rang. Lieutenant Haas snatched it up. "Haas here." He listened with a face devoid of expression and an eye stuck on the chief. The chief stared at his desk with a longing. Finally Lieutenant Haas said, "Yes, I understand, and thanks. Get back to me when you can tomorrow . . . Yes, this number." He cradled the receiver. His eye had never left the chief. "It wasn't a drowning," he said.

The chief waited. "All right, what was it?"

"The exact cause still isn't definite, but he came up with a slug. Twenty-two caliber."

The chief did not react, as if the grim truth were not all that important. His hands were no longer in his pockets but hanging loose.

"I think you're going down the tubes, Chief. Do you still want to stick to your story?"

Except to shift his weight, the chief did not move. He stood silent, and, as if on signal, the two troopers reentered the office. He suspected they had come in for the kill and

81

would arrest him. For young giants, they seemed strangely bloodless. They had soft pudgy faces, each with eyes, nose, and mouth clustered too close together. Sergeant Cox was not with them. The chief sensed they had told him to go home. Lieutenant Haas stirred.

"Your story, Chief. Sticking to it?"

His only thought at that moment was of his mother-in-law, of her horrified reaction at seeing him escorted out of the station, probably in cuffs. He said, "Yes."

Lieutenant Haas smiled. "You're a cool customer."

The telephone shrilled. A part of the chief jumped. The troopers immediately hovered, breathing down his neck. The phone shrilled again, and finally Lieutenant Haas lifted the receiver. The chief hoisted a hand and ran it over his chin. He wondered whether his mother-in-law knew what was happening and whether Wilbur Cox had really gone home. The detective named Mack nudged him with knuckles.

Lieutenant Haas, hypocritically polite, said, "For you."

The chief tipped forward. His hand was too moist for the receiver, which nearly slipped from his grasp. As he struggled, Lieutenant Haas vacated the desk and joined the troopers, their voices muffled. The three of them moved to the door. With utter surprise, then with rage, the chief noted their departure. They had tried a bluff, and it hadn't worked.

Alice Cross gazed in on him. "Are you talking to somebody?"

The chief raised the receiver. "Hello."

A voice said, "Get over here."

Outside in the lot Lieutenant Haas jingled his car keys. He said to the detective named Mack, "What do you think of him?"

"Horse's ass," Mack said.

Lieutenant Haas turned toward the other detective. "What do you think of him?"

"Horse's ass," concurred Hector.

"That's been my opinion," Lieutenant Haas said. "But I could be wrong."

Mack said, "I thought you were going to sweat him more."

"There's always tomorrow."

Hector said, with a grin, "He didn't much like you sitting at his desk."

"It was the wrong move," Lieutenant Haas said, casually observing a movement in the shadows between two cars. "It got him angry. I wanted him scared."

"I think he was."

"He was both scared and angry. A wrong combination."

Mack unbuttoned his jacket. "If he's not a horse's ass, what is he?"

"The Lone Ranger," Lieutenant Haas said. "Except he can't trust Tonto."

"Who's Tonto?"

Lieutenant Haas spoke in a louder voice to the shadows. "That's you, isn't it, Sergeant?"

Sergeant Cox made himself visible. "I don't have to take that shit."

Lieutenant Haas gave his keys a final jiggle. "Of course you do. If you want to be chief."

Mack walked the lieutenant to his car and, opening the door for him, murmured, "It's the same thing, isn't it? A horse's ass and the Lone Ranger."

Lieutenant Haas climbed into his car and harnessed himself. "Not always."

It was nearly midnight. For the second time that day Chief Jenkins visited Ed Robertshaw's fishing shack. This time the chief went inside. The decor was polished oak and burlap of an expensive cut. The lighting was subdued, the lamps of a sportsman's design from L.L. Bean. Ed Robertshaw's bald head looked as solid as granite. His swimming trunks lay wet in the sink, flung there. He was wearing a checked robe, loosely cinched. His jaws were shiny, freshly razored, raw and bleeding in places. The chief recognized it as a brutal act of shaving to think terrible things out. The illegal nighttime swim was probably a challenge to the elements and to the shark if there was one. Ed Robertshaw dug out two bottles of Labatt's ale from the fridge.

"Sit."

The chief moved to a small round table of blond oak, and Ed Robertshaw joined him, clinking down two bottles, no coasters, no glasses. A breeze stirred the burlap curtains. Ed Robertshaw sat carelessly, his belly billowing out and his genitals reposing in his lap like a dish of false fruit. The chief looked away, embarrassed. Without thirst, he tasted the ale.

Ed Robertshaw said, "Amy's a wreck. My sisters are doing what they can for her." He watched the chief run a finger down the bottle. "Don't do that. I hate it when people peel the label. Tells me something about them I don't want to know."

The chief ceased and desisted.

Ed Robertshaw said, "Is it murder?"

"The medical examiner found a bullet," the chief said.

"I know all about it."

"Then why'd you ask?"

"Don't get flip with me." Ed Robertshaw's eyes glinted. He covered his lap. "I'm sorry Lyman's dead but not sorry he's gone. You see the difference?"

The chief looked at him. "Yes."

"He didn't turn out the way I hoped. Actually I never had

any real expectations, since he was already a loser. You know what I mean. But Amy wanted him, and I let her have him. My mistake, and I paid for it. He squandered his family's money and lived off mine. The house he and Amy lived in, the food they ate, the whole marriage, that was one big wedding gift from me."

The chief already knew this and said nothing.

"My daughter put up with more than any woman should've. He turned her into an emotional cripple years ago. I paid for the shrinks. I'm still paying." Ed Robertshaw's voice had taken on an odd quiver, and his eyes had sunk back. "I don't want my daughter suffering anymore. You follow?"

The chief was uncertain. He felt he wasn't thinking fast enough, which irked him. Ed Robertshaw drank from the bottle, a healthy swig.

"Your sergeant got through to me. The shit-shoveler says you're covering up for your old friend. Any truth in it?"

"None," the chief said.

"She had her hooks in Lyman once. Don't tell me she's still got them in you. No matter how you cut Winnie Wallace, she's no prize."

"That doesn't make her a murderer."

"What does it make her, Paul? Just a piece of local tail? Tell me."

The chief let his head sway. "I only know there are things going on I don't understand."

"That's obvious. First the dentist and then my son-in-law—unthinkable for a town like this. Unthinkable that it should affect my family." Ed Robertshaw's face widened, and his eyes disappeared into their hollows. "If you've lied to me, I'll burn you. Do you doubt me?"

The chief did not doubt him in the least.

"I appointed you. I can dump you."

"I've always known that."

Ed Robertshaw snapped his fingers. "I can do it this minute without a reason."

"You've always been fair to me, Ed. Why are you being unfair now? It's not your way."

"You don't know what my way is. I'm the only one who knows my way."

"Should I put myself on notice?"

"No. I'm just reminding you of your position."

The chief sighed. "What do you want from me?"

Ed Robertshaw made to rise, projecting mystery. "When it comes time, you'll know."

"I don't understand."

"You don't have to. Get out."

Chief Jenkins walked through the dark to the Ford. His leg bothered him. Not the bad one, the other one. The door of the shack opened behind him, and light shot out, the ray almost reaching him. Ed Robertshaw shouted.

"Paul. I'm not myself."

The chief half turned. "Yes. I realize that."

"Bear with me."

"I have no choice."

Pamela Comeau was sleeping soundly in an upstairs bedroom. She had taken something.

Laura Kimball was downstairs in a deep chair, her long legs extended. Her high cheekbones picked up light from the only lamp burning in the room. She had stuck a marker in the book she had started, Nadine Gordimer's latest, and the book had slipped to her knees.

Joan Weiss was in the bathroom, where the fluorescent glow was ghastly. One of the tubes flickered. The window was raised, and the ocean was a distant whoosh. Someone out in the dark whistled for a dog. Joan had on a sweatshirt, the sleeves rolled up. Her shorts, at this time of the month, were tight on her. She undid them and, reaching for a small floral box on the glass shelf, busied herself. She was halfway finished when something alerted her. Her head snapped up and her eyes leaped to the window. "Damn you!" Her voice was choked with outrage, and her cheeks burned, as if something unsavory had kissed them. *"Damn you!"*

Laura was asleep in the chair. Joan did not disturb her. She swept by her, almost upsetting a vase of cut flowers. She paused out on the porch but saw nothing. She heard a sound, perhaps the jingle from a dog collar. The only other sound, as she tripped down the porch stairs, came from the sharp swells of the surf.

She sprinted through the dark, the sand squeaking underfoot like packed snow. A wind off the ocean galloped at her. Colored in intensity, accompanied by the beginning of a roar. Stumbling, she cursed Winnie Wallace for never having warned them about jet airplanes bombing overhead and of lecherous men protruding into their lives. Hetty Nelson's cottage lay ahead.

The cottage was unlit. The door was unlocked. The old woman had few fears. Pushing the door open, Joan called her name. She pawed around for the light switch and, failing to find it, groped through the kitchen to the bedroom.

"Hetty, it's me. Joan Weiss."

Then she realized the face was not Hetty Nelson's but a man's. He was sitting on the edge of the cot. She went rigid.

Hetty Nelson, buried under covers, said, "It's all right, dear. It's just Bud."

Joan tottered. The odor of souring things from the sea rose up in the darkness. She made out the shape of Bud Brown's hands and sensed his heavy torso. Her outrage overwhelmed her fears, and she pointed a trembling finger. "You were looking in my window!"

Bud Brown's face faded. Hetty Nelson spoke invisibly from her pillow. "He didn't mean anything by it. You should've just ignored him."

Joan let out a hateful cry. "Not when I'm pushing in a tampon!"

The chief said, "Tell me everything."

"Everything? What's everything?" Winnie Wallace was subdued, introspective, not quite the same person as before. They were sitting in the Ford in her dark driveway. She had hurried out of her house when she had seen the headlights, which he had flicked off as soon as she had slid in beside him. Her breath was stale from cigarettes. "Make up something for me," she said, "and I'll swear to it."

"Listen to me," he said, frowning into her shadowed face. "They'll be questioning you soon, you and everyone else at that party. They'll round you all up, do you understand?"

"I'm not worried."

"Then why should I worry about you?" he said with an edge.

"Because you care for me. You always have."

He let his head fall back for a moment and listened to the traffic on the boulevard, no large trucks allowed, but he heard one sneak by. "Let's try to get your story straight," he said. "You followed Lyman out on the porch. Why'd you do that?"

"Because he followed her. I knew what he had in mind."

"Yet up to that point you'd had no contact with him."

"He avoided me."

"But you kept an eye on him."

"It seemed the thing to do."

"All right," the chief said with a sigh. "What happened on the porch?"

"He was being ugly with her. It would've got worse."

"We're talking about Mrs. Comeau."

"I've already told you all this."

"Tell me again. Keep telling me." His voice was relentless but soft. The night air was rich with sea smell, and he watched her lift her face to it. "Why did you butt in? Maybe Mrs. Comeau could've handled the situation herself."

"Maybe," she said without conviction.

"All right," the chief said with another sigh. "She left the porch, and you stayed with Lyman. Then what happened?"

"I told him to leave. He wasn't wanted. And I told him to take the Smiths with him. You know what that was all about, don't you? Three-in-a-bed stuff."

"Aren't you guessing about that?" the chief said after a pause.

"It was a good guess. It struck home."

"Did he leave?"

"I think so, I'm not sure."

"Why aren't you sure?"

"Because I left."

The chief's voice tightened. "Winnie, you didn't get to my house until nearly dawn."

"I didn't plan to see you at all. I came here first. I made my way down the bluff."

"In the dark?" He looked at her with exacting scrutiny. "How could you do that in the dark?"

"I don't know, but I did," she said indifferently. "Then I waded into the water. I'd have gone skinny-dipping, but the surf was rough. Instead I sat on a rock."

"You were there a long time."

"Yes. Do you believe me?" When he did not answer, she

turned her head to free herself of his eyes. She smiled grimly. "I was twenty when Lyman dumped me. Now look at me, Paul. Long in the tooth."

He had nothing to say. She looked at him.

"Why didn't I marry you? Tell me."

"No," he said. "You tell me."

Ten

Sergeant Wilbur Cox sought out the town clerk and, after some negotiation, was grudgingly given a key to a large unused room behind the tax collector's office. The sergeant lugged in card tables, chairs, and rickety portable partitions and neatly arranged the room into cubicles, the proper privacy for individual interrogations. Lieutenant Haas, flanked by the troopers, viewed the creation and said, "Fine. I want them coming here in twenty-minute intervals, husbands and wives together when possible. I don't want this taking any more time than it should."

"Right," said Sergeant Cox. "I've got Officer Morin ready to ride out to those I can't reach by phone. I don't see a problem."

"Save the Wallace woman for last."

"I already figured that."

"You set up four cubicles. We only need three."

The sergeant's face fell. "How come?"

"Three is enough."

Sergeant Cox gave a fleeting unforgiving look at Hector and Mack and said, "Why them and not me?"

"Because," Lieutenant Haas said quietly, "they know exactly the kind of questions I want asked. I've trained them."

"You saying I don't know the kind of questions to ask?"

"I'm saying I haven't time to find out."

Sergeant Cox drew himself up, seemed set to say something sharp, and then merely ran a hand across his chin. He

91

left the room unhappily. The trooper named Hector said, "I can see that guy giving us trouble."

The one named Mack said, "He doesn't look all that bright."

"You're both right," Lieutenant Haas said and moved into one of the cubicles and sat down. He looked at his watch. It was a little after nine. "If we're really lucky we'll be done by noon."

"You don't expect much?"

"I expect everything."

The district attorney was on the phone early, a call to Concord, the Republican Charlie. "Hope I'm not bothering you at breakfast, but Boar's Bluff is really busting for me. It looks like another murder."

"Yes, I'm reading about it in the *Monitor*."

"*Union-Leader* has a bigger story. And both Bostons have it on page three. Channel Nine had it last night."

"Are the killings related?"

"We don't know for sure at this point, but they seem to be. I was thinking, Charlie, I might arrange a big press conference. What do you think?"

"Depends on what you're going to say."

"Just something general."

"Did you speak to Ed Robertshaw like I asked?"

"Yes."

"What'd he say?"

"Said he'd get back to me."

"Has he?"

"Not yet."

"Then wait. You don't know which way the wind's blowing yet. If you still have ideas about going for governor, you'll need people like him."

"Yes. Maybe you're right."

"How are you feeling, Chugger?"

"Fine."

"The heart?"

"I know what you're asking. I'm fit as a fiddle. I wouldn't snow you."

"Good. Keep in touch, Chugger."

The fidgety woman, birdlike and bespectacled, leaned confidentially over the card table and said, "Between you and me, lieutenant, it was a boring party. I really expected much more."

"Why?"

The woman flashed a smile. "The hostesses seemed a cut above others who give parties here. My problem is I've seen much too much of the world. I was an army brat, you know."

Lieutenant Haas placed his pencil on his note pad. "Thank you for coming down."

"That's all? My goodness, you didn't ask me much." She rose. "I should mention he rather did have his eye on me too."

"Yes, thank you for your time. On your way out would you ask Mrs. Comeau to step in?"

In the next cubicle the trooper named Hector propped a heavy elbow on the card table and said to Joan Weiss, "You mean he crashed the party?"

"No, not at all. I simply said we didn't invite him. The Smiths brought him."

"So you didn't know him."

"That's correct," Joan said.

"You never set eyes on him until he showed up with the Smiths."

"Actually I saw him on the beach that day. We spoke briefly."

"How did that come about?"

"He approached me."

"Out of the blue?"

"You meet all sorts on a beach, even a semiprivate one."

"Like the dentist."

"Yes," Joan said, staring him in the eye. "Like the dentist."

The other trooper, Mack, used a grubby handkerchief to wipe his neck. The breeze from the single fan in the room did not reach his cubicle. He was sweating, and Laura Kimball was not. He jotted down on his pad: *Cool customer.* "You and your two friends are here for the summer alone? No husbands?"

"We're divorced."

"No children with you?"

"My two daughters are grown. They're college students and have summer jobs. The same is true for Mrs. Weiss's son. Mrs. Comeau has younger children, but they spend their summers with their father in Seattle."

Mack was quiet. He studied the patrician line of Laura Kimball's face, which was much too interesting to be beautiful. It was asymmetrical, quiet-eyed, thoughtful, long-boned. It confused him. He said, "You don't look old enough to have kids in college."

"Thank you."

"All the same, you can't be forty yet."

"Exactly forty."

He wrote on the pad again, *divorcees,* the script tiny for such a huge hand. "Do you entertain much?"

"Hardly at all. That was our first party here."

"You're Boston people," he said in a way that indicated disapproval.

"Yes. I live in the Back Bay."

"Where all those fires were."

"That's the South End."

"That's right. Back Bay's the ritzy section."

"Only parts of it. Mrs. Weiss lives in Cambridge, Mrs. Comeau in Brookline."

"I guess what I'm getting at is you and your friends didn't know anybody in Boar's Bluff till you came here."

"Not a soul."

"How'd you happen to rent that house?"

"Classified section of the *Boston Globe*, summer rentals. Wallace Realty."

"You didn't know her before?"

"Miss Wallace? No."

Mack doodled on the pad. His jacket was off and his sleeves were pushed back. When he ran a forearm across his mouth, he sipped his own sweat. His upper lip glistened. "What's your opinion of her?"

"I have none."

"Why not?"

"I don't know her well enough."

He doodled on the pad. "So you neither like her nor dislike her."

"Actually," Laura Kimball said without a pause, "I rather like her."

A while later Mack poked his head around the corner of Hector's cubicle and asked in a heavy whisper, "You think the lieutenant would mind if I took a quick break? I need a Coke."

"I think he wants us to work straight through."

"That's what I was afraid of."

Hector returned his gaze to the Smiths, who were sitting quite close together, like lovers. "Sorry for the interruption," Hector said, his eye focusing on Mrs. Smith, who had been responding to most of his questions. "I was wondering why Mr. Arnold's wife didn't go to the party. I mean, why not the four of you instead of just the three of you."

"Amy Arnold doesn't go to parties. She doesn't go anywhere." Mrs. Smith looked at her husband. "Does she, darling?"

"No," said Mr. Smith, who sat pigeon-breasted in his turtleneck jersey. He struck Hector as someone who worked hard not to disturb himself. "She's rather withdrawn."

"I see." Hector clicked the head of his ballpoint pen several quick times. Mrs. Smith smiled tolerantly through peach lipstick and lit a Virginia Slim. There was no ashtray. Hector said, "How long did you know Mr. Arnold?"

Mrs. Smith gave her husband another glance. "How long have we been coming to Boar's Bluff? Six years? Seven?"

"Closer to ten."

"That's how long we knew him," Mrs. Smith said, and her eyes suddenly filled. Her husband swiftly reached for her hand, the one holding the cigarette, and nearly burned himself. Mrs. Smith spoke with a breaking voice, a tear smearing her cheek. "He was a beautiful person. Wasn't he, dear?"

Mr. Smith took an ash on the knee. "He was Number One."

Lieutenant Haas tried to conduct quick and concise interrogations, all questions piercingly on target, but Hetty Nelson frustrated him. She rambled on about her brother whose body had washed up near the same spot where Lyman Arnold floated in. The lieutenant was interested until he realized the drowning had taken place more than a half-century ago.

She was not sure of the year.

She passed gas and excused herself. "I'm rotten with age," she explained. "That's my problem."

"That's all right," Lieutenant Haas said with restraint.

She stood up. "I used to be bigger. I've shrunk, you know."

"Sit down, Miss Nelson." He was gentle but firm. He had an aunt her age in a nursing home. Hetty Nelson sat down, fanning her face with a spotted hand. She wore a bonnet.

"I've been alive so long I need a bookmarker for my mind. Where were we?"

He told her. His patience was professional. His aunt in the nursing home was a nuisance.

Hetty Nelson said, "First let me tell you Lyman Arnold was no better than the dentist. They were two of a kind, cut from the same cloth."

"I think we've established that."

"Except," she said, reconsidering, "maybe Lyman Arnold was worse because he married someone nice. The second time, I mean."

Lieutenant Haas brightened, and his prominent eyes reached out. "I know what you're saying."

"What am I saying?"

"His first wife was Winnie Wallace. She's not so nice." The lieutenant smiled. "You picked up on her the last time we talked. You had a lot to say. Remember?"

Hetty Nelson was slow to nod, as if she had misgivings, and the lieutenant leaned his face toward her over the table.

"Let's pick up on her again."

"I've said enough," Hetty Nelson murmured and passed more gas.

"Come on," Sergeant Cox said. "I'll buy you a tonic."

Officer Leo Morin consulted his watch. "I should be checking the beaches."

"Plenty of time for that." Sergeant Cox guided Officer

Morin past the town clerk's office and down the corridor to an old-fashioned Coca-Cola machine that dispensed bottles instead of aluminum cans. The sergeant deposited coins, and a bottle thumped free. He opened it and passed it along.

"Thanks." Officer Morin tipped his cap back and looked no more than fourteen years old. Gulping from the bottle, he looked twelve. He was twenty-six. Wiping his mouth, he said, "Aren't you having one?"

"Can't drink the stuff. Sours my stomach." Sergeant Cox drew closer, confidentially. "I heard what she did to you."

"Who?"

"Alice Cross. Making you go up a tree for a goddamned cat."

"Yeah." Officer Morin took another swig. "I could've broken my neck."

"Degrading. If she wasn't the chief's mother-in-law, she couldn't get away with that crap." The sergeant hooked a thumb inside his belt and produced a dead smile. "I'll tell you something, Leo. We've got a bigger problem than her. The chief himself."

Officer Morin inclined his head, his eyes wide, as if an element of perversity had been introduced into the conversation. He increased his grip on the Coke bottle.

"It's a problem you could help me with. It involves keeping an eye on him. That scare you?"

"I don't know. I don't even know what you're talking about yet."

"A cover-up."

"What?"

"Come on," Sergeant Cox said, placing a firm arm around him and easing him away from the Coke machine. "I'll tell you about it."

★ ★ ★ ★ ★

"I guess that's it," Hector said. "Except for the Wallace woman. I guess you'll be talking to her yourself."

Lieutenant Haas nodded. "Where's Mack?"

"Getting himself a Coke." Hector had his note pad in his hand. He flipped back some pages and said, "I think Mrs. Smith was extra friendly with the victim."

"Which one was that?"

"Plump, in her thirties, kind of pretty. She and her husband were the ones brought Arnold to the party."

"Was she also on that list I showed you for the dentist?"

"No."

"But you think she might've been nice to Arnold."

"A gut feeling."

"What's her husband like?"

"A piece of toast."

Lieutenant Haas did not appear interested. He said, "Wallace should be here pretty soon. While I'm talking with her I want you and Mack to do something special for me."

Hector grinned. "I can see it coming."

"Can you do it?"

"Sure."

Footsteps sounded in the corridor, and Mack appeared in the doorway with a girl, lanky and barelegged, her breasts crushed in a halter-top that was too tight. "Excuse me, Lieutenant, but the young lady here has something to tell you."

Lieutenant Haas gave her a leisurely look, mildly reproving. "What's your name?"

"Charlene Farnham." She gazed down at her sandaled feet. "I don't want to get anybody in trouble."

"Who don't you want to get in trouble?"

"Excuse me, Lieutenant, but she says she saw Chief Jenkins on the beach the other night meeting someone from the party, someone he was waiting for. A woman."

"Let her speak for herself, Mack." The lieutenant's eyes bore into the girl. "Is that right, miss?"

"Yes, sir."

"Who was the woman?"

"I couldn't tell."

"Come in, miss. Come in and sit down." He turned to Hector. "Wallace comes, make her wait. Take Mack with you and tell him what's up."

"Right."

Lieutenant Haas twirled a chair around and sat in it backwards, something he hadn't done in years. "Okay, miss. Tell me who you think it might have been."

The district attorney was chatting with cronies in the hallway of the Exeter courthouse when his secretary tapped his shoulder and whispered that he had a call from Concord. Charlie. He rushed to his office and grabbed the phone. "Yes, Charlie. Anything the matter?"

"Ed Robertshaw contacted me."

"He called *you?* He was supposed to call me."

"He knows me better. Prepare yourself. What neither of us knew is that the second victim was his son-in-law."

"Jesus!"

"No love lost between them. The guy did nothing but chase ass, according to Robertshaw. He wants you to proceed with the investigation any way you see fit, even if it touches his police chief."

"I'll be damned. I didn't expect it to be so easy."

"By the way, I told him about your ambition. He may become your biggest supporter—money and manpower."

"Charlie, this has gone unbelievably well. You're beautiful."

"He does have a suggestion. He wonders why there has to be two murders. Why one isn't enough for your purposes."

The district attorney went cold in the chest. "Just a minute," he said, rising. He went to the door and closed it. Slowly he returned to his desk. He picked up the phone and said, "Charlie, Jesus Christ!"

"I guess he's thinking of his family, the scandal and all. He thought maybe it could be a drowning."

"Impossible. The medical examiner has already ruled that out."

"The paper mentioned a possible shark attack."

"Charlie, there was a bullet."

"What bullet? I didn't read anything about that."

"We haven't released that information yet."

"The medical examiner's a friend of yours, isn't he? If he isn't, he should be."

The district attorney put a hand to his head. "Do you know what you're asking me?"

"Chugger." The voice was stern, the tone a reprimand. "I'm not asking you anything. Ed Robertshaw is."

"He's asking too damn much."

"In a way, Chugger, much as I hate to remind you, so are you."

"What do you mean?"

"Do you have any idea how much it costs to become governor?"

Chief Jenkins was at his desk. He was studying Sergeant Cox's work sheet, which indicated many hours of overtime, a problem since the department was not budgeted for it. When he looked up, he saw Lieutenant Haas gazing in, eyeballs extended.

"It's late, have you had lunch yet?"

The chief said, "I don't eat much during the day."

"I'm the same way, especially when I have a lot on my mind." Lieutenant Haas advanced into the office and took a chair. He seemed as crisp and neat as he had at the start of the day. His silk tie was one of his brighter ones. He said, "Your friend Wallace was good. Nervous but good. What made me think of lunch was that her stomach kept growling."

The chief initialed the work sheet and pushed it to one side. "Did her answers satisfy you?"

The lieutenant half smiled.

The chief said, "Did you ever think you might be dead wrong about her?"

"It would be nice for you if I were."

"You're convinced you're not."

"I keep an open mind," Lieutenant Haas said and turned in his chair at the scrape of footsteps. Hector hovered in the doorway. Mack was behind him. The lieutenant's eyes stretched toward them expectantly, but their expressions were negative. He concealed his disappointment and dismissed them with a nod.

The chief, though curious, said nothing.

The lieutenant, as if forced to play a card too soon, said, "I understand, that night, you were on the beach with a woman. Was it your friend?"

The chief spoke coldly. "It was Mrs. Weiss. Didn't she mention it?"

"Not that I know of."

"She must've thought you already knew."

"Because you'd have told me?"

"Yes."

"Why didn't you?"

"It wasn't important."

"Why were you meeting with her?"

"I wasn't *meeting* with her. She was taking a breather from the party, too much noise, smoke or something, and we met by chance."

Lieutenant Haas was contemplatively silent for a long moment. Then he said, "Yes, I'll buy that. The real question is what you were doing on the beach."

"It's not unusual."

"Really." Lieutenant Haas seemed fascinated. "Were you also on the beach the night the dentist got it?"

"I doubt it."

"That's an answer?"

"Do you find something wrong with it?"

"You scare me, Chief. You really do. I wonder if you'd be willing to take a polygraph."

"Go to hell."

Eleven

Cora Dray spread boxes from the better shops over the bed and opened them all, the contents a contrast of hot and cool colors. She reserved a skirt of burnt-orange to try on first. Her dress removed, she stood before a full-length mirror and pinched the flab of her upper arms. Her plan was to lose weight, the reason her new clothes were a size below a normal fit. She glanced glumly at her boiled thighs, knowing she was stuck with them. She would die with them that way. Suddenly she screwed her head around. Though she saw and heard nothing, she knew her brother lurked behind the partly closed door. She detected his body static, which clashed with hers.

"There'll be none of that," she said sternly and sensed his backing off a bit. "If you're going to live here now, you're going to act like a man. A real one."

There was no response.

She said, "I know you're there."

"What makes you think I want to live here?" The tone was petulant, with the eerie whine of a child, a sudden and almost savage regression.

"Because I say so," Cora Dray said, with much of the Mommy in her voice. "Go downstairs. You make me nervous."

"I'm hungry."

"I'm not making anything now. I'm busy. Go to Philpott's."

"I don't have any money."

After rummaging about, she extended a hand past the door's edge and fluttered three nearly new dollar bills that smelled of her pocketbook. She felt her brother's breath on her fingers. "Stop that," she said irritably. "Take it and go!"

Later, tightly wrapped in new colors, the zipper giving at the side of the orange skirt, she picked up the telephone, carefully, as though it was a weapon. When the ring was answered, she disguised her voice by deepening it. "You slut. You filthy slut." There was a hard silence from the other end, so she went on. "You'll get yours. Believe me!"

In a barely audible voice, Winnie Wallace said, "I know who this is."

"Good," Cora Dray said and crushed the phone down.

Charlene Farnham's mother was in Philpott's buying milk, and Chief Jenkins was near the newspaper rack. She tried to avoid him, but he saw her and smiled, which embarrassed her. The plastic jug of milk she carried was burdensome, and she shifted it from one hand to the other as she stumbled toward him, every married year of her life incised in the sparse flesh of her face. "I'm sorry," she said.

"What are you sorry about, Agnes?"

She glanced about to make sure nobody could overhear. "Charlene shouldn't have talked to the State Police like she did. She had no right saying what she did, not after all you've done for her. There's a lot I'm not supposed to know, but I do." Agnes Farnham's voice quavered. "That terrible business with the dentist. You could've dragged her into it. Instead she's trying to drag you."

"She's a kid."

"The rest turn out like her I don't know what I'll do." Agnes Farnham rested the milk on a stack of unsold *Union-*

Leaders. "The town's lucky to have you, Chief. We know you look after us, and some of us appreciate it."

The chief's smile was a shade rueful.

"Even him," Agnes Farnham said. "You even look after him."

Bud Brown had entered the store and seated himself at the snack bar, his shoulders softly hunched, an inert presence waiting to be fed.

"Sometimes, when I'm washing up, I know he's out there. I can feel his eyes right through the shade. I don't mind. It's the kids I worry about."

"He wouldn't hurt anybody."

"I know that. And he's my only admirer. Maybe I like it."

"I wouldn't advise telling him," the chief whispered.

"No. That would spoil it. Might even scare him off." Her eyes crinkled, and for an instant some of the years fled her face. "Why do I say something to you I'd never say to my husband?"

"Because I'm the chief," he said, thinking that he was joking and then realizing that he was not.

"And," she said, "because there's something about you that lets it happen."

"The only problem is sometimes you think you know somebody and later find out you don't."

"Who are you talking about, Chief? My Charlene?"

"No." He lifted the jug of milk for her. "Myself."

The regulars at Philpott's, occupying stools where the counter curved into the wall, watched Bud Brown eat and then leave. The man wearing bicycle clips blew on his coffee and said from the side of his mouth, "He gives me the creeps. He always did."

The man beside him, who had just gotten a haircut and

smelled it, said, "Whether he killed his brother-in-law or not, the chief oughta lock him up just in case. My wife's keeping the doors locked. I have to knock to get in."

"The chief's not in charge. The Staties are."

"Then what are we paying the chief for?"

"You tell me."

"What I wanta know," a third man said, using a knuckle to adjust his dentures, "is why no one's said definite yet how Lyman Arnold got killed. Because I'll tell you right now that's shit about a shark. No sharks around here."

The man with the clips said, "He could of drowned."

"Or he could of been murdered just like the dentist," the man with the haircut said. "That's what my wife heard."

The man with the dentures bit into a brownie and chewed with a mysterious smile. "You boys wanta know what I heard?" He chewed some more. "I heard the chief's protecting somebody."

"Who?"

He showed mock surprise while wetting a napkin. "Who do you think?"

"Jesus. Who told you that?"

He removed his upper plate and wiped it clean. "Wilbur Coxth. He thaid not to thay anything."

Pamela Comeau was on the telephone pleading with her ex-husband in Seattle. "Please," she said, "let me speak to one of them."

Laura Kimball was trying not to listen.

Joan Weiss was out on the porch absently pulling dead leaves off the hanging fuchsia. Her attention fixed on a Coast Guard cutter floating beyond the feathered waves. It was searching for a shark. People were on the beach, but nobody was in the water. Joan turned with a jolt when someone uttered her name.

Winnie Wallace appeared at the porch steps. A smile was carved unnaturally into her face. She came forward hesitantly, and Joan regarded her with alarm.

"What's wrong?"

"Nothing." She chucked a cigarette butt over the rail. "Do you know what that boat's doing out there?"

Joan nodded.

"I've never seen a shark. Have you?"

Joan nodded again. "Something is wrong," she said.

"I need to ask a favor."

Joan was on guard. "What is it?"

"I don't want to be alone."

Chief Jenkins went home in the afternoon and slept fully clothed on his bed. It was still light when he awoke, but a cooling wind through the pines was sweeping into the room. Slit-eyed, he jacked himself on an elbow. Then he gave a fierce start. "What the hell!"

"Take it easy." Lieutenant Haas sat in a chair carried in from the kitchen. His usually smooth hair was sticking up in back. "You snore, Chief. Miss Wallace ever tell you that?"

"I could arrest you for breaking and entering."

"The door was open."

"What do you want?"

"You may be off the hook. If you're smart."

The chief sat upright on the bed, stuffing pillows behind him. "Nobody's ever cited me for my intelligence. Naturally I resent it."

"You want to listen or not?"

"I'm listening."

"I was wrong about Arnold taking a bullet. The M.E.

never did find one. The other night I misunderstood him. Or maybe I heard what I wanted to hear. We all tend to do that from time to time."

"I don't believe you," the chief said.

"You want it in writing?"

"You'd better keep talking. How did Arnold die?"

"The M.E. still isn't sure. When there's doubt, things take longer. He says there's a chance Arnold died of terror. His heart stopped cold when the shark hit him. Or he could've bled to death."

"How do you explain the fact he went swimming with his clothes on?"

"He had alcohol in his blood. He was drunk. His death could even be termed 'misadventure.' "

The chief inspected a thumbnail, picked at it, and then bit it. "I think I'm beginning to get the picture."

The lieutenant's smile was small and defensive. He seemed smaller and slighter, vulnerable like everybody else. "We each have our masters, don't we? Mine's in Exeter. Yours plays games here out of a fishing shack." He got to his feet. "The first homicide still holds. I want Winnie Wallace. That's what gets you off the hook and me out of your town."

The chief swung his stockinged feet over the side of the bed and stood up unsteadily. "She's not mine to give."

"I want the weapon," Lieutenant Haas said, all his self-assuredness returning. "I want that fucking little pistol she's hiding."

"You're presuming a hell of a lot."

The lieutenant moved to the doorway. "Go back to bed, Chief. Sleep on it."

He didn't sleep. He shaved and showered, ate his supper from a can, and watched television. Twice he heard unfamiliar noises from the outdoors. Once he went to a window. Lightning bared the ground, but no rain fell. Shortly before midnight the phone rang.

"I thought you might be worried," Winnie Wallace said in a small voice. "You've probably been trying to call me."

"Yes, I have," he lied. "Where are you?"

"I'm at the gray house. They're letting me stay the night."

"Why? Why should you want to?"

"I need to, Paul. I got a crank call today. I pretended I knew who it was, but I didn't. Everybody's after me."

"Change your number. Get an unlisted one."

"I can't. I'm in business. Paul, there's more. Somebody—people—were in my house while I was at the Town Hall being questioned. They went through my things. Everything, even underwear. Neatly, but I could tell. Paul, what were they looking for?"

Another of those unfamiliar sounds from the outdoors filtered in, and for a moment he held the phone away from his ear. Someone or something was out there. He said, "A small-caliber pistol. If they'd found one, they'd have left it there and come back with a warrant."

"Good God!"

"Maybe I'd better come after you."

"I know what you're thinking. But I'm not imposing. They'd tell me if I were." The quality of her voice changed. "Besides, I like being in the company of women. For a change."

"As long as you know what you're doing."

"I think you said that when I was seventeen, the first time you took me parking."

He was not sure who disconnected first. Probably it was she. After slipping on his desert boots, he went out onto the tiny porch and watched the pinpoint explosions of fireflies.

There were no more flashes of lightning, only the threat of rain and droppings from the pines. The chirr of insects seemed all of a piece. When he suddenly flicked on the overhead light, he looked toward the pines and saw a face visibly engraved against the dark.

His shoulders sagged. He felt betrayed, though he knew he should have expected it. "Leo, get the hell off my property!"

The young officer's frightened face vanished.

The chief stood crookedly, as if absorbing pain, and in time he heard a car start up on the road and speed off. It was going to be a bad night. The chief could feel it.

From her dark bedroom, Cora Dray heard her brother pull his car into the drive, but she did not hear him enter the house. She was curious but not enough to investigate. She was in a mild mood of depression that threatened to sustain itself and perhaps grow. Her side of the bed was hot and messy from where she had lain flat on her stomach with a hand buried beneath her, a finger twitching and producing not the powerful result she was accustomed to but a feeble one, not enough to count. She rolled to the cool side and reached for the telephone. Push buttons lit up. She knew that the minister's wife retired early and that the minister stayed up reading, writing, sermonizing to himself. She pressed out his number. When he answered, she said in a throaty voice, "Your wife's no angel."

The minister was more of the other world than of this one. He said, "Are you sure you have the right number?"

"I'm sure." Her hair had been dismantled and washed. It felt silk-soft against her neck and shoulders. "Your wife should wear a scarlet letter."

The minister was silent. She pictured his babyish face, mild and milky and puckered at the mouth.

111

"I'm doing you a favor telling you."

"I don't think you are," he said in a clerical tone. "Nor are you doing yourself one. Is this who I think it is?"

"Who do you think it is?"

He hesitated. "I'd rather you tell me."

"I'm a parishioner." She spoke wryly, flexing her flat feet under the covers, the nails scratching the sheets. "I need solace. Would you care to come over?" Her mouth moved closer to the receiver, making her voice hard to understand. "If you were here right this minute, you'd have a treat."

"I can't hear you," he said, and she slowly repeated the words, alarming him. "You need help. Perhaps somebody else's rather than mine."

"Yours will do. You still want me to reveal my name?"

He was silent, as if he had changed his mind.

"Winnie," she said. "Winnie Wallace."

A few moments later she padded downstairs to her dead husband's liquor cabinet. She felt she richly deserved a small brandy. Also it would help her sleep.

Winnie Wallace left the unfamiliar bed and ghost-walked in her borrowed gown to the bathroom, where she used the john, weighed herself, and inspected the medicine cabinet. A bottle of One-A-Day Vitamins fell into her hands. She unscrewed the top and swallowed two tablets, after which she gargled with Listerine, rubbed Raintree Beauty Lotion into her face, and squirted a dab of Delfen Contraceptive Foam onto the back of her hand, a moment later rinsing it off under the tap. Closing the cabinet, she stared at three toothbrushes and wished there were a fourth, hers beside theirs. An intimate arrangement. The sort she remembered from summer camp, giggling girls flashing baby breasts and exaggerating experiences, that sweet and silly interlude before the deeper disenchantments. When she left the bathroom, her mouth wore a light mist of lipstick, frost-colored.

Joan's door was shut, as was Laura's, but the next one was ajar. She pushed the door open enough to slant in a cone of light. "Are you awake?" she whispered and edged in. A salty breeze aerated the room. A floorboard squeaked. Bedside photographs of children, beautiful faces emerged from the shadows. Another beautiful face stared up at her from a pillow. "Can't you sleep?" she asked.

"I haven't tried," Pamela said.

"I hope I didn't scare you."

"I know every sound in this house. Even yours now."

"May I?" Winnie sat on the bed, flesh tones surging through the gown. Her breasts were well-defined, her stomach delicately stuffed. She eyed the photographs. "The girl is you. Spit and image. She must be special."

"They both are."

Winnie's tongue slipped across her icy lips, honing the edges. "Was the father a bastard to you?"

"The bastard was Roger."

"Who?"

"Somebody else." The voice was quick. "He's not important anymore."

Winnie lifted her legs onto the bed and tucked them beneath her. The breeze in the room was cool but humid, and her bare belly wetted through her gown. It made her feel large and yeasty. "I haven't been smart about men either. Actually, it comes down to what you know about yourself. Too much and not enough, if that makes sense."

Pamela lay quietly under the sheet but with some evidence of tension in her eyes.

Winnie Wallace said, "I like talking to you. I don't know how you feel."

113

"I don't mind."

"Do you have sisters?"

"Joan and Laura."

"I mean real ones."

"They are real."

"I guess you know what you're saying. Realer than real." She sat back on her hands, dust in her underarms. She had stopped shaving there. "I'm used to being alone," she said with a non-aggressive air of independence. "I mean, it doesn't bother me as long as I can reach out when I like and touch somebody. I usually pick on Paul. The police chief."

Pamela raised a slim wrist and looked at her watch, the hour ghostly. She was silent.

"Would you rather I not talk about him?"

"It doesn't matter."

"We can talk about anything, nothing. So much doesn't have to be said."

"What does that mean?"

"I don't know myself. I often say things I don't quite understand." Winnie smiled, showing white and sturdy teeth. "I was poking in the bathroom. I guess you heard. Who uses foam?"

There was a moment of incomprehension and then a weary sigh of fatigue. "It's ancient. It's probably gone bad."

Winnie leaned forward. "I like what you're wearing. What is it?"

"A shirt-dress," Pamela murmured, elevating her head a little and immediately letting it drop back, as if the pillow demanded it.

"Go to sleep if you like."

Pamela already had. She slept for two or three minutes and opened her eyes gradually. Winnie lay beside her under the sheet, an arm thrown tenderly over her.

"I'll leave if you like."

After several seconds, Pamela said, "One of us had better shut the door."

The Farnham's dog, as sleek as it was black, trotted through lamplight onto Mrs. Myatt's lawn, where it stopped, crippled itself, and forcefully fouled the grass. Then it straightened, stiffened, and kicked up sod. Bud Brown stood motionless watching from the distance, where day lilies, clenched in the night, were poised like daggers. The dog growled, bounded over the intervening space, and came forth at a slower gait, chops open. The eyes were small and brilliant. Yellow. Bud Brown spoke softly, reached out, and patted its bony head. They were friends.

The dog followed him to Ocean Boulevard, where he tried to make it go back. It wouldn't despite a hiss and a push. It scampered across the road on swift paws, its nails tapping the pavement, its collar jingling. Now it was Bud following the animal, to the beach, where they soon separated. The ocean groaned, and the dog raced toward it. Bud aimed himself at the gray house.

He gazed up, a faint flicker of light determining his choice of a window. He mounted the porch. His feet were silent. He climbed atop the rail near the fuchsia and probed a post that held a heavy protruding nail, a foothold. He knew the nail was there because one winter he had hammered it halfway in. With body English, he ascended to the roof and angled into position. He heard a rustling. He peered through the screen of the window and for a split-second panicked, convinced that a woman was giving up her ghost. Then he saw that it was two women, one leaving the bed of the other. But his first impression lingered, and he edged back over the shingles, as if death had to be kept at a great distance.

Dangling a foot, he found the nail and lowered himself to the rail, his shoulder disturbing the hanging plant. For a frightening instant his balance was precarious. Tottering and recovering, he had the chilling suspicion that someone was zeroing in. Moments later he was off the porch and on the sand. The dog was there. So was Sergeant Wilbur Cox, an immobile presence in the dark.

"Let's walk."

They tramped away from the house, Bud pitched forward, soaking in his own sweat. Once he stumbled, and the breath jerked out of him. The dog followed.

"Come here, boy," Wilbur said, removing his revolver. The pearl handle flashed. He hammered the animal on the skull with such force that it went down on all fours without a sound.

Bud began to cry, softly.

Wilbur said, "The chief lets you get away with this shit. I don't."

Again the pearl handle flashed. Repeatedly.

Twelve

The dog dragged itself home in a light predawn rain. Whimpering, it crawled under the rusted camper in the drive and died. Bud followed. On Ocean Boulevard he weaved and pitched and went down on his knees, but on Lodge Road he stayed on his feet, clutching at things for support, a tree, a low fence, a prickly shrub. Several times he thought he heard his sister call him in a child's voice. He used all his remaining energy to climb into the camper and close the double doors behind him. Folding his arms fetally and rolling on his side, he listened to the rain on the roof and sought sleep to dream away the bad. Quite rapidly he lapsed into a coma.

Sergeant Wilbur Cox overslept. Several times his wife came into the bedroom and shook his shoulder, and each time he slapped her hand away and fell back to sleep. She hung a fresh uniform where he would see it and gathered up the crumpled one he had left on the floor. She saw blood on the front of the shirt and more on one sleeve, as if he had stuck his arm in a bucket of it. Lightly, without disturbing him, she lifted the sheet to look at his body. There was not a mark on it.

She descended the basement stairs with the uniform draped over an arm. Two of her children started to follow her down, but she waved them back and made them close the door. The basement was damp and cool. She switched on both the washer and the dryer and let them vibrate to the fullest. Water pipes knocked and rattled. With an eerie air of calm, she began to scream.

Wilbur Cox pounded down the stairs on bare feet, the oldest daughter behind him. Gladys Cox was still screaming, though not as loud. When she saw them, she stopped, exhausted. He said, "What the Christ is the matter with you?"

She said, "You're killing people."

"You dumb shit!" His daughter tried to stop him, but he spun her aside and lunged at his wife. He slapped her with open hands, back and forth, not as hard as he could, for he, in another way, was also exhausted.

Winnie Wallace showered, using a cake of soap almost too large for her hand, and dried herself in a towel that was a little damp. Someone had already used it, which she had known when she had snatched it up, though a fresh one had been left for her. She stepped on the scale and was pleased when the needle fluttered only a pound past her desired weight. Making fists, she pummeled her abdomen, already as firm as it would ever be, the bulge insignificant. She looked in the mirror and was surprised by her eyes. They were full of puzzlement, as if over herself. When she crept downstairs, Joan glanced up from the *Times*, sections spread over the table.

"There's coffee if you want it."

"I do." Cups had been laid out. She picked one up and turned to fill it. "We the only ones up?"

"Oh, no," Joan said. "Pam was up first and went for a walk. Laura's on the beach."

"How is she?"

"Laura? Fine."

"Pam?"

"She has a migraine. That's why she went for the walk. Sometimes it helps." Joan began putting the *Times* back together, carefully, so that it looked as if it had never been peeled. "It's Laura's," she explained. "She doesn't like the pages ruffled."

"You three look out for one another."

"We try."

Winnie sat down with her coffee. "I won't be staying long. I think I'm going to sell a house today. I can feel it."

"I wish you luck."

"Some houses are easy. They have a vitality about them and sell before you even get the For Sale sign up."

"Do you have many of those?"

"I've had my share." The coffee tasted pleasantly of chicory, but Winnie did not fully enjoy it. Her hand trembled, and she put the cup down fast. "As a realtor, I give myself high marks. I'm clever, usually, and I work hard, also usually."

"Why the qualifications?"

"Life's full of them." She was talking nervously for the sake of talking. "I hate to see a house painted pastel. Houses shouldn't ever be cute. They should be solid. Handsome. Warm. Don't you agree?"

Joan did.

Winnie tried lifting her cup again, this time with a more confident hand. "Do you people work?"

"Yes. Of course." Joan was amused. "Though we manage to get our summers off. I do public relations, freelance. Laura teaches. Pam's a secretary."

"That's all she is?"

"That's all a degree in medieval history could get her."

"I thought you might have money of your own."

"Laura has a little. Actually I do, too."

"Pam?"

"I really don't know. She might."

Winnie finished her coffee or at least all that she intended to drink. Placing a hand on the table, she lifted herself up. "I'm wearing somebody's underpants. They were drying in the bathroom."

"They must be Laura's."

"And actually these shorts aren't mine."

"Laura's, too, I think."

"Not Pam's?"

"No."

"Just as well," Winnie said mysteriously.

"I'm sorry." Joan gave her a confused look. "Am I missing something?"

Winnie's voice, meant to be light, came out doleful. "No, not a thing."

A young man in a stained smock said, "You're not supposed to be in here."

Closing the door quietly behind him, Chief Jenkins said, "I know that." He was in the basement of the Exeter hospital, inside the morgue. Intensely fluorescent, it reminded him of something else, the untidy kitchen of a restaurant. There were too many utensils scattered about, too many knives capable of separating bone, too many pans and trays holding milky and meaty substances. He looked beyond the young man.

A third voice said, "What do you want?"

"I'm Chief Jenkins. Boar's Bluff. We've met before."

The medical examiner concentrated on his work, a butchered body lying with its innards out. "Yes, what do you want?" he asked, hunching over the parts like a vulture. The chief kept his distance.

"Is that the Arnold autopsy?"

The medical examiner looked up. He had a red face like a

welt and too much loose skin under the chin. Amused, he said, "This is a woman." His right hand was sheathed in rubber, the other was bare. The bare one pushed away limp hair from his face. "I don't usually see much of you."

"That's true," the chief said in a tone that almost didn't carry. He gazed at a beaker of discolored urine, purplish, and wondered whether it came from the woman. He knew it was urine because someone had scatologically tagged it *pee*. He did not suspect the young man in the smock, who appeared foreign-looking and humorless.

The medical examiner said, "Do you want a look at Arnold? Depends upon your stomach."

"No. But I'd like to talk to you about him."

"Sure," the medical examiner said and shot a glance at the young man in the smock, who caught the message and left. The rubber glove came off with a squeak. Naked fingers fluttered. "What do you want to talk about?"

"I understand there's no bullet," the chief said maintaining his distance.

"You understand correctly. What's the matter with you guys? Doesn't the right hand know what the left one is doing?"

"I just wanted to hear it from you."

The medical examiner instantly went on guard, eyes full of suspicion, wariness. "What the hell's going on here? Do you have an argument about anything?"

"No," the chief said with a wounded sound. Certain chemical odors emanating from all sides were getting to him.

"Because if you do, I'll get the phone right now and tell the D.A. all bets are off. I don't need this kind of aggravation."

The chief's hip bumped against the dull edge of a steel table, and he felt the pain all the way down to his trick knee. His wife, he remembered, had been brought here, and a man not unlike this one had cut her up. Perhaps her urine had been drained into the same beaker.

"Are you here on your own?"

"Yes," the chief said in a frozen way. "It was a mistake."

"I still don't like it. You worry me."

"You don't have to worry."

"I've got myself to think about."

"I understand," the chief said. "I shouldn't be here."

"You're damn right you shouldn't." The welt of a face had blossomed bright, but the intent eyes were relaxing. "I know who pays my salary, and I guess you know who pays yours."

The chief backed away, a hand blindly seeking the door. "Do me a favor. Forget you saw me."

A small crowd gathered. Officer Leo Morin pulled up smartly in a cruiser. All the Farnham children were there, including Charlene, wearing a T-shirt bearing the call letters of a rock radio station. She stood with an arm around her mother while her father leaned forward, his scalp thrusting through the tattered gray of his crew cut. Years of hot work in sheet metal shops, mostly the Portsmouth area, had taken bits and pieces out of his face. He murmured, "We had him since he was a pup."

Mrs. Myatt, with a grim air, as if justice had been done, retreated to the rear of the crowd and said to no one in particular, "I'm glad it's dead. Last night it did business on my lawn."

Ken Farnham ran a hand over his rough face and said to Officer Morin, "I just happened to look under. Then I dragged him out."

Officer Morin said, "Looks like somebody clunked him on the head."

"I'd like to clunk the bastard that did it."

Cora Dray heard the commotion, and somebody told her that the Farnham's dog was dead. She despised the Farnhams, considered them trash. Her feelings had extended to the animal. She walked down the street and scanned the crowd. She was looking for her brother, annoyed that he was not in the house when she had gotten up and puzzled that his car was still in the drive. She made a face and turned back.

Officer Morin said, "Somebody might've been trying to get into your camper."

Ken Farnham gave out a short bitter laugh. "It don't even run."

Officer Morin stepped close to squint through a side slit of soiled glass. After a number of seconds he whispered, "Jesus," and staggered back. "Somebody's in there."

Ken Farnham jumped over the carcass of the dog and grappled with the rear doors, his fingers almost too big for the handles. "Come out, you bastard!" he shouted as Officer Morin yanked out his revolver and almost dropped it. People pulled back, confusing Mrs. Myatt, who skittered to one side. Two of the smaller Farnham children screamed.

Cora Dray, halfway home, heard the sounds and stopped in her tracks. "Bud," she whispered to herself, as if from a vision of him, and began retracing her steps, weaving, trembling, her pace much too slow. She saw golden spots before her eyes and her brother, aged four or five, raising the cut pad of his hand for her to kiss.

Cars appeared, slowing, stopping. She crossed the street. The crowd had regrouped and grown, but people readily yielded to her. Then someone tried to hold her back, but too late. She saw the upper portion of her brother, the face a fearsome mask of dried blood. A voice spoke hurriedly to her, "It's all right, Mrs. Dray. He's not dead."

"Not yet, you mean," she said and felt herself floating away. Somebody caught her.

Chief Jenkins drove back from Exeter. At times Linda Cross Jenkins materialized in odd places. Once, while he waited for gasoline at Skelly's Mobil, she leaned out of a car bearing a Connecticut license and sought directions from Skelly as if she were a stranger in her own town. Another time he glimpsed her through the glass in Philpott's, where she clung to a young man's arm. It was as if she had not died but had picked up new existences. Now, abruptly, he saw her again, a solitary figure in a sun dress on the rural roadside.

He slowed the Ford. She had a swift city stride, a propelled pace, and she did not see him until he pulled alongside her. She shied back. "Don't be afraid," he said, at once realizing his mistake. The Ford idled roughly. "I'm Police Chief Jenkins."

"I know who you are."

"You're Mrs. Comeau."

"Yes," she said. His eyes fixed on her in a way meant to establish immediate intimacy, a habit of his. It disquieted her, and her face, shining with perspiration, rayed out her distrust. "Were you looking for me?"

"No." There was a bit of a ditch behind her, a birch stretching over it and wildflowers blooming on the edge. "Be careful." He wanted her to come forward, but she stayed where she was. "Have you walked all this way?"

She nodded, her blond hair wet where it fringed her forehead. "I was about to turn back."

"Would you like a lift?"

She shook her head, something building up in her. She took a tentative step to walk away, maybe even to run. The chief suspected he was terrifying her, as he had once terrified his wife by accidentally discharging his revolver. That was the last time he had fired it. He tried to appear as benign as possible.

"Is Miss Wallace still at your place?"

"I don't know."

"It was nice of you to let her stay the night. Some people can take her only in small doses." Immediately he felt traitorous for putting it that way.

"It wasn't my idea."

"Probably Mrs. Weiss's. She must be a pushover."

Pamela Comeau took another small step away from him. Her lips were sun-cracked. She seemed more vulnerable than a moment ago.

"I'm sorry," the chief said for no clear reason other than for having stopped and bothered her, though he was glad he had. She was no longer looking at him. A station wagon had drawn alongside the Ford, a little beyond. It had Massachusetts plates. A man and a woman were in the front, and children crowded the back. Viewing the chief suspiciously, the man poked his head out.

"Everything all right, Miss?"

Pamela Comeau gave an uncertain nod.

"Can we give you a lift?"

She glanced at the chief. "I'm sorry, but this town frightens me." She skipped briskly around the front of the Ford to the side of the station wagon. A door opened, and she squeezed in with the children. The chief watched silently.

He was somber, as if miscast for the role he was playing.

Thirteen

Cora Dray would not leave her brother's bedside in the intensive care unit. A nurse, checking the gauge on the oxygen tent, worked around her. Her brother's face was mutilated and ballooned, painted, tubes running out of it. His head was shaved and stitched and half covered with small-adhesive bandages easily removed. His left ear, if he lived, would need to be reconstructed. Machines monitored him. A curtain provided privacy. Somebody bumped the curtain, and Cora Dray glanced sharply at the nurse.

"Is that the doctor?"

The nurse looked past the curtain. "No." She was large and ungainly but nimble in executing her duties. Her white uniform glared. "How are you doing?"

"I'm not leaving," Cora Dray said and received no argument. Presently the nurse left. Cora Dray reached under the covers and touched her brother's arm, the one with nothing needled into it. By closing her eyes she could pretend nothing was the matter with him. By keeping them shut she could silently scold him. She opened them when the curtain rustled. The doctor looked down at her.

"You shouldn't touch him."

"He's mine to touch," she said but withdrew her hand. She rose deliberately from her chair and stared at the doctor, who was too young for her to trust. "Tell me," she said.

"Not here."

She had no choice. She followed him past the curtain, out

126

of the ICU, and into the corridor. When he continued on, she said, "This is far enough," and forced him to turn back and face her.

"I thought you might like coffee," he said.

"No. Tell me," she said, taking a breath. She did not like his looks in the least. He was short and had fuzz for hair, like a baby's. His mouth tended to pucker, again like a baby's. The only thing she considered adult about him was his three-piece suit. "Is my brother going to die?"

"You're thinking the worst."

"No. The worst is he'll be a vegetable. When are you operating? Why are you waiting?"

"The clot may dissolve. We'll know better tomorrow."

"I want a second and third opinion."

"I've given you a consensus," he said tersely and looked at his watch. "If you'll excuse me."

"Aren't you staying?"

"They'll call me if there's a change."

"I want you here!"

He gave her an impatient look. "I have a family, you know."

"I don't give a damn about your family!" she said, startling him. Her shoulders were shaking. "They mean shit to me. It's my brother that matters."

The doctor retreated and vanished down a stairwell. She leaned against the wall for support. Then she bent over a bubbler and drank, letting chunks of water strike her face, for her skin was burning. When she looked up, she saw Chief Jenkins emerging from the stairwell the doctor had descended. He approached with a limp, his second trip to the hospital in one day.

"They'll pay," she said, looking at him and then through him.

"They? Who are they, Cora?"

"All of them."

"You're not making sense." He extended a sympathetic hand, but she avoided it. Her eyes were righteous.

"Everyone will pay."

"Think about it," Lieutenant Haas said. "That's all I'm asking." When he received no reply, he said, "Did you hear me?"

The chief nodded. He was slouched behind his desk, his legs thrust wearily to one side. The laces on his desert boots were loosened. Lieutenant Haas sat on the edge of the desk, conspiratorially, and smiled only with his eyes.

"One homicide. That's all we've got on the books. This would take care of it." The voice was deadly low. "Am I getting through to you?"

The chief rubbed his face, pressing the flesh under each cheekbone until it hurt.

"It takes your friend off the hook," the lieutenant said. "That's what you want, isn't it?"

"It takes everybody off the hook."

"That's right. You included."

The chief felt his stubble and wondered how old he looked. "Bud Brown's not your man."

"You don't know that."

"Neither do you. What if he lives?"

"They can't cut. I checked with the doctor. The clot's in a tricky place. If he hangs in, the best they can do is keep him on life support."

"I also checked with the doctor. The clot could dissolve."

"One chance in a thousand. He tell you that?"

The chief looked at the ceiling, which was streaked where water had once leaked in, a particularly bad winter rainstorm.

The chief remembered it well. Alice Cross had strategically placed buckets on the floor and one on his desk. He said, "If he dies, it's another murder."

"Unrelated. You can handle it. I've done enough."

The chief attempted a smile. "I'm surprised. You were so hot on my friend. Why aren't you now?"

"You said it yourself. She could go to pieces." The lieutenant coiled an arm behind his back and scratched. "My boss and yours both think she might confess to too much."

"What if I told you I was wired? Every word recorded?"

The lieutenant smiled with an open mouth. "I'd say you were a horse's ass."

The chief sighed, "I'm not wired."

"I know you're not. Maybe I know you better than you think."

"Maybe you'd like to introduce me to myself."

The lieutenant's smile held. "I'll leave that to you. The best time is when you're alone."

"You're quick."

"I have to be. I cover a whole state. All you've got is a town."

"I don't see why you even bothered to consult me."

"We want your cooperation. Your boss told mine you'd give it. If you don't want to, that's your decision."

"You don't sound like a cop." The chief's chair creaked. "You sound like a politician."

The lieutenant colored. "I'm a better cop than you'll ever be and smart enough to know some cases you close the best way you can, with whatever comes along. Face it Chief, this Bud Brown suddenly became a natural. I saw it right away. Didn't you?"

"Like you say, you're the better cop. But I've got a question for you. What if somebody else ends up dead from a twenty-two-caliber pistol?"

The lieutenant eased himself off the edge of the desk and stood straight. "The first thing you do, like I already told you, is get hold of the weapon. The next thing you do is throw it in the ocean."

Wilbur Cox came out of his house gripping a can of beer. He had on old pants and a sweatshirt hacked off at the shoulders, which made his arms look heavier than they were, more powerful. Pollution greased the air. He had been burning rubbish, which was illegal. He said, "What are you doing here?"

The chief's Ford was parked in the dirt drive, and the chief stood on sparse grass. "I was worried."

"I called in sick. Didn't Alice tell you?"

The chief's eyes watered, and he rubbed them. "What are you burning?"

"Trash. You want me to pay a fine or something?"

"Smells chemical."

"That's what trash is."

"Are you burning clothes, Wilbur? Maybe with some bad stains on them?"

"What kind of question is that?"

"Just a question." The chief gently shifted his weight. It was one of those rare times he was wearing a revolver. It was wedged in the waist of his chinos and covered by his loose shirt. "I suppose you've heard about Bud Brown."

"I hear he's in real bad shape. Might not make it." Wilbur Cox swigged beer, Budweiser. The can was sweating. "I'm surprised someone didn't lay into him a long time ago, the way he sneaked around looking in windows. Imagine how much ass he must've seen!"

"Did he ever look in your windows, Wilbur?"

"He wouldn't have dared." The sergeant extended the beer can. "You want to hit on this?"

The chief shook his head. "Right now it's a brutal assault. If he dies, it's murder."

"I don't know what murder is anymore, Chief. Not after the Arnold case. I guess that was something decided by the higher-ups. Don't worry, Chief. I know enough to keep my mouth shut."

"I'm not worried, Wilbur. I'm only concerned right now about Bud."

"You should be. You're going to draw heat. People think you should've locked him up years ago for his own good. You babied him, Chief. You shouldn't have done it."

"There's some truth in that," the chief said with a slow nod of concession. "But, I'll tell you what really bothers me. I keep remembering the time you got in a fight with a guy from Pease. Granted, it was a while ago. At Peter's Place. You were just back from Vietnam, still in uniform. You went at the fellow with a bottle. They had to pull you off him because you wouldn't stop clubbing him. He almost died."

"It was self-defense. He was a nigger, and he was doped up, AWOL, and had a blade. What's that got to do with Bud Brown?"

"I know how you feel about him. I might as well tell you that Lieutenant Haas is laying the Dray homicide on him."

"What?"

There was irony in the chief's eyes, all of it directed at himself. "I remember Haas saying at the outset that these things are usually tied to someone in the family. Bud's his man. The dentist's case is closed."

Wilbur Cox was deadly still. He had much to fathom and took his time, and then, slowly and confidently, began to smile. "Sure, why not? Wraps it up real nice."

"Except for what's happened to Bud. Level with me, Wilbur. Did you do it?"

The sergeant was suddenly enjoying himself, the ground so much firmer now beneath his feet. "Maybe I did, maybe I didn't. You're never going to know."

The air was still and tepid, the evening sun pink-red. Listlessly lifting his shirt, the chief exposed his revolver and regarded it curiously, almost with surprise. "Why did I bring this, Wilbur? It must've been to arrest you, but I guess I can't."

"I don't like a guy whistling through his ass, Chief. Makes me nervous."

"Is that what I've been doing?"

"You bet." The sergeant's enjoyment was immense. He drained the Budweiser can, crumpled it, and threw it on the brown grass.

"You're fouling your own nest," the chief said.

"The wife will pick it up later. That's her job."

The revolver was now in the chief's hand. He wasn't pointing it at anything, merely gripping it with loose discomfort. "Pick it up," he said clumsily and released the safety. Sergeant Cox seemed amused, as if he were being entertained.

"Where are you going to shoot me? Between the eyes?"

"In the groin," the chief said in the manner of a man no longer bent on winning, only on breaking even. In a flash, Wilbur Cox retrieved the can. The chief squeezed the trigger. *Click.* He squeezed it again. *Click.* "I never load it," he explained.

"You son of a bitch!"

Wilbur Cox lunged. The chief whipped him once with the revolver.

★ ★ ★ ★ ★

On the open patio of a cottage well beyond the gray house, a half-dozen women nursed weak drinks and watched the sky redden and the beach empty early. One said, "What's their rush?" and another said, "Can't you guess?" A third offered, "No one wants to be out there after dark. I know I don't." A fourth spoke with agitation. "I feel the whole summer's been poisoned." She scratched the top of her tan thigh and left streaks of chalk.

Four of the women were seasonal residents, and the other two were year-round and lived past a craggy bend in houses of weathered shingle. Most wore bathing suits of leaf pattern, and one looked like a perfect Avon lady under a wide-brimmed hat. Their deck chairs groaned as they rearranged their legs and spoke in spurts.

"Our back door doesn't lock right. Henry's fixing it."

"I didn't know he was handy."

"He's learning fast."

"We have a window won't go down all the way."

"Use soap."

"We tried."

A woman large and yeasty said, "I hear a noise in the night, I jump."

"You're not alone."

One of the women depleted her drink and the woman whose patio it was got up and provided a refill. "Anybody else?" she asked and made the rounds with a pitcher. "Maybe I should add more vodka."

"No thanks. We want to stay alert."

"Damn right!" came a supporting voice. "What scares me is it's probably somebody we see every day."

"I don't like any of that bunch that hangs around Philpott's. They all look goofy."

"It could be somebody from Pease."

"It could be a beach bum. Somebody hopped up, Henry says."

"That's a thought."

"I don't trust anyone anymore."

"Speak of the devil."

A man in tangerine shorts approached the patio. It was Henry. He had heard the last bit of the conversation. "I'm with you," he said in hushed tones. "If we weren't paid through Labor Day, I'd pack up and go home."

The last rays of the sun were maroon, and then shadows shot over the beach. From the porch of the gray house Laura Kimball peered into the spreading dark and said, "Somebody's out there."

Joan Weiss was beside her, and Pamela Comeau, swiftly joining them, clutched the rail. They had dined on lobster. Broken shells rose jagged and sharp from a bowl on a portable table behind them. A modestly priced bottle of burgundy glinted empty. Her voice strained with anxiety, Pamela said, "Man or woman?"

"Shhh," Laura said. Her legs looked like quivering poles beneath her shorts. Her eyes were not keen.

"It's not a woman," Joan said.

"It could be anybody, nobody," Laura said and, in a failing attempt at levity, offered, "It could be my ex-husband impersonating a man." As the words fell flat, so did her face. "He got away with it for years, didn't he?"

"Probably just a kid," Joan said and expected to make out the fermenting features of some teenager. The figure was soft-footing diagonally toward the house and growing less anonymous as it penetrated the light hazing off the porch. A lean man gazed up. Joan, recognizing him, said, "Hello."

Chief Jenkins' face, bitten clean by a razor, was luminous, which made him seem strangely like a suitor. Instinctively the women tightened their expressions. "It's only me," he said.

"What do you want?"

His gaze went to Laura, who peered down impersonally at him from her long legs. He said, "You're the only one I haven't met yet."

Laura nodded. "How do you do."

Joan said, "If you're looking for Miss Wallace, she's not here."

"In a way I am," he said. "I have good news for her."

"We haven't seen her since morning. We don't expect her back."

The chief's feet shifted in the sand. He appeared vaguely forlorn as he clumsily advanced a pace, as though he were on foreign soil, an American preparing to produce proof of identity and a statement of worth. "I wonder if I might join you."

Pamela shrank back. Joan said, "Officially or unofficially?"

"Unofficially."

"It's late, Chief. Some other time."

In a dream Pamela shared the bed with Roger, a man she often told herself she had never known, could not possibly have known. Stirring against her, he elongated his lips for a kiss. Then the dream curved in on itself, and every breath hurt her. His spit flew with questions she could not keep up with. "What are you going to do? Tell somebody? Tell who? The police? Who'll get hurt the most? Me, you, or your kid? Have you thought of that?" Her wrists went numb where he gripped them, and his voice hammered her. "Huh? Huh?"

She woke up gagging and hoping no one would hear. The hour was small. Blindly she hung a hand over the bedside phone as if she could pick it up and dial the dead, her favorite grade school teacher for one, her grandmother for another. With a chill she considered the possibility that a wrong ring would resurrect Roger. Again she gagged, this time into her hand.

Light stabbed her eyes. Joan and Laura had opened the door and were peering in with alarm and concern. They did not know everything she had been through with Roger, but they knew enough and advanced immediately to the bed. They smoothed the covers, tucked her in, treated her like a child. It was not what she wanted but at the moment what she needed.

"Go back to sleep," Joan whispered and set her mouth, a sign of strain. Laura hovered.

"We can stay if you like."

Pamela shook her head. For the moment she felt purged, and she looked waxen. Her smile was small but ghastly.

"Cry, Pam, cry," Laura said gently. "You never have."

Fourteen

A white Corvette floated in between the pumps and the station. Drawn and sleepless, Cora Dray peered out from behind the wheel. The two women knew each other slightly. Cora Dray frowned a little. Skelly spoke first.

"Is he going to make it?"

"I don't know what he's going to do. His head isn't his anymore. A machine's keeping him alive."

"Can he feel the hurt?"

"How do I know? I can't ask him." Cora Dray narrowed her eyes. "He means something to you, doesn't he?"

Skelly wiped her hands on her coveralls. She did not like to admit anything. "You drove up, I thought it was him. Like nothing had really happened."

"You and I," Cora Dray said, "we're the only ones who care. Doctors don't give a damn."

"I don't want him hurting."

Cora Dray lifted up a copy of the *Union-Leader*, statewide circulation, the district attorney's picture displayed under a headline that proclaimed *Murder suspect may never stand trial*. No photo of her brother. She'd refused to give one out. "They've already convicted and buried him."

"He never did harm. Only looked in windows."

"Tell that to our police chief."

"He knows."

"Sure he knows. But he doesn't care either."

Skelly had no color in her face except for a pink splotch on her forehead. It was a small signal, scrutable only up close, that she was agitated. "Who beat on Bud? I want to know."

"I don't know." Cora Dray's lips were a coarse color. "Why? What would you do?"

"The same that was done to Bud."

"That's what I wanted to hear," Cora Dray said. "Because I've got other scores to settle."

The district attorney visited Ed Robertshaw at his Strawberry Drive home. They sat on a colonnaded veranda overlooking birch and pine. One of Ed Robertshaw's sisters served decaffeinated coffee and then left them alone. The district attorney, gray-skinned and chain-smoking, said, "My friends call me Chugger, Mr. Robertshaw."

"Call me Ed," Ed Robertshaw said easily. "Someone told me you married a Templeton. We've got Templetons here in Boar's Bluff. Good stock."

The district attorney was instantly more at ease. "Thank you," he said.

"Tell me honestly, Chugger, what do you think of your chances? Be realistic."

"I'll know better in a month or so, but I definitely feel I have a shot."

"If you've got Charlie up in Concord behind you, you've got more than a shot. Of course there'll be the issue of your health. How's your ticker? Those cigarettes don't help it."

The district attorney nodded with a guilty smile. "These are low-tar."

"You ought to get out in the sun more. Get yourself some color."

"I've bought myself a lamp."

"I don't trust lamps. The sun's natural." Ed Robertshaw ran a hand over his bald head, which was charred. "The previous governor of New York greased his hair red. Made him look nice on camera."

"I think he did that for a woman."

"That's what politics is, Chugger. It's like courting. You do anything you have to to win the bitch."

The district attorney, who had married above himself, said nothing. He tasted his coffee and watched sparrows spring from one birch to another and then swoop onto the grass. Gently he cleared his throat. "I'm sorry about the tragedy in your family. I'm just glad I could help out a little. How is your daughter doing?"

"She's a Robertshaw. She'll come through."

The district attorney chose his words carefully. "It doesn't look as though this Bud Brown character will make it."

"Just as well, wouldn't you say?"

"Yes. It's nice to have everything cleared up, though there's always the danger of loose ends. I hate to have something come back to haunt us."

"The best thing about dealing from a position of power," Ed Robertshaw said, "is that you can make things happen . . . or unhappen." He glanced up as his sister reappeared to ask whether they wanted more coffee. "No," he said authoritatively. "The district attorney is just leaving."

"Oh," Miss Robertshaw said, and the district attorney, confused, rose lopsidedly from his chair. Miss Robertshaw smiled kindly at him. "It was nice meeting you," she said. She was a plain woman, nothing to look at, and the district attorney did not look at her. He shook Ed Robertshaw's hand and waited for something to happen. Nothing did. With an angry sense of betrayal, he prepared to leave. He took a step, then another.

"I almost forgot," Ed Robertshaw said in a whimsical tone and produced a white envelope thick enough to be significant. The district attorney took it with a look of relief and quickly buried it inside his suitcoat. It was the first contribution to his gubernatorial campaign.

The minister's wife had a hair appointment in Hampton and was readying to leave when the telephone rang. She snatched it up before it sounded a second time. The voice of the caller was undisguised, or only half disguised, as if total effort weren't worth it. "Pippy, please."

The minister's wife recoiled. Only family members and very old friends were in the habit of calling her husband by his childhood nickname. "I'm sorry," she said. "He's not in."

"Where is he?"

"He's at a meeting."

"Do you know who this is?"

"Yes, Cora. I'm so sorry about Bud. Is there anything I can do?"

"You've done enough, don't you think?"

The minister's wife felt sick, as if she'd taken a blow to the belly, and the scent of her lipstick became nauseating. She put a hand to her mouth.

"I've lost everything," Cora Dray said in a deadly tone. "My husband and my brother. And now the police are pretending my brother's a killer. What d'you think of that?"

In a few years, no more than five, the minister planned to retire to rural England, birthplace of his grandparents. The minister's wife wished they were there now.

"The police chief," Cora Dray said, "is protecting his whore, or maybe he's protecting you, I don't know."

Truly, for that instant, the minister's wife wished that she were dead.

"I'll call back," Cora Dray said menacingly and rang off.

The minister was home. He was in his study. He emerged

from it in his shirtsleeves, the church newsletter in his hand. "Who was that?" he asked.

"My hairdresser," the minister's wife said. "She can't take me."

It was late afternoon, and people were deserting the beach. Pamela Comeau, sitting on a towel in her sleeveless robe, was one of the few to remain. She watched two children gouge the sand with toy shovels and suffered from the sight, for the children reminded her of her own at that carefree age. Now, at fourteen, her son was cynical and dour, and her daughter, sixteen, was permanently bruised. And they were far away from her. A jet flew over, dragging its sound.

She got to her feet.

The breezy near-emptiness of the beach disconcerted her. Someone called to the two children who reminded her of her own, and with regret she watched them scamper away.

She imagined a path in the sand and followed it. The ocean was receding, and she tramped over the dregs, stopping short when a chill passed over her. The air had changed. She shivered and looked around.

Up in the heart of the sand a man sat hunched over raised knees behind a folded-back magazine. He was not in a bathing suit or even in shorts but in regular clothes, and he had been watching her. She saw a quarter of his face, enough to identify him.

It was the police chief.

She had her towel in her hand. She dropped it. Her legs weakened, fine legs that were betraying her with each step she took. She was trying to return to the gray house and was not in the least confident she would make it.

She tripped climbing the high porch steps and dented a shin. The pain was ferocious but not enough to stop her.

When she reached the top she glanced quickly over her shoulder but couldn't see anything. The sun blinded her. She hobbled into the house, where she expected voices to soothe her and arms to comfort her. A note was on the table. Laura Kimball and Joan Weiss had taken the Volkswagen and had gone for groceries on Route One.

Up in her room where the silence welled into certain hums, ticks and chinks, she sought a state in which everything about her would be external, mechanical. Minutes passed. She examined the damage to her shin. Her head jerked up when she heard a rap on the downstairs screened door, and then she heard somebody setting a foot inside the house. The chief called her name.

She crept out of her room.

In her hand was a small-caliber pistol. It was nickel-plated and still reeked of cordite from the last time it was fired.

Crouched on the landing, she could see him, but he could not see her. She saw the part in his hair, the stretch of his neck, and the sweat stains in his shirt. The biggest one was across the chest, which was where she aimed.

"You dropped your towel," he said. "I'll leave it on the table." His eyes searched for her. "Did you hurt yourself?" he asked, and something in his voice saved his life.

Fifteen

Gladys Cox kept her distance, forcing Cora Dray to climb out of the Corvette and to trudge in high heels over the uneven lawn. A septic smell emanated from the rear of the property. Cora said, "I could never understand what Stephen saw in you. You're not even pretty."

Gladys trembled, flanked by two of her children.

"You're probably not even clean. He could have infected me."

"Please." Gladys Cox's lips quivered. "You can say what you want to me, but not in front of my children. Kids, go see Laurie."

The children didn't budge, as if their function were to protect their mother. Distastefully Cora said, "They don't look healthy."

"They're healthy."

"And they don't obey."

"Kids, do as I say."

They complied, all of a sudden racing away on spindly legs as their mother watched. Cora's high black hair seemed to swell in the heat. Her blouse was a mosaic of hot colors, a few buttons left loose. Cleavage showed. She let a silence build and then dramatically sighed. "Does your husband know?"

Gladys stood numb.

"Cat got your tongue?" Cora asked, slicing a smile through her words and gaining satisfaction as the younger woman aged before her eyes.

"Please."

"Please what?"

"Don't tell him."

"Are you begging?"

"I will if you want." Gladys dropped to her knees.

"Stay there," Cora said. "That's where you belong. I didn't know everyone Stephen took up with, but I'm sure you were the lowest."

"Are you going to tell?"

Cora came back with another sharp smile. "Maybe I will, maybe I won't. I'll let you sweat it out."

The district attorney smoked three different brands of cigarettes. He started off the day with Benson & Hedges, switched to Winston Lights in the afternoon, and in the evening smoked mentholated Kools. His wife listened to his coughing, a horrible sound, as if he were breaking bones in his chest. She was in the kitchen. He was in the den watching television. She knew she was going to lose him. She just hoped it would not be too soon. Another five years, she thought, was not asking too much. But she knew she was being unrealistic.

She entered the den with a tumbler of water and an assortment of pills for his heart and blood pressure. He gave her a look that was loving and accepted the water. She dispensed the pills one at a time. Afterwards, he lit a Kool. There was no way she could make him quit or even cut down.

"How are you feeling?"

"Tip-top," he said.

She sat beside him, the Exeter *News Letter* lying ruffled between their chairs. The television was tuned to a movie each had seen before. She said, "Did you get the money?"

He nodded.

"You don't look pleased."

"It wasn't as much as I was expecting."

"After what you did for him!" She was shocked. "How much?"

"He fooled me with a thick envelope. Small bills. Came to a thousand."

"I warned you." Her husband always confided in her but did not always follow her advice. She had cousins in Boar's Bluff, and not one had a good word for Ed Robertshaw, a man with too much local power, a monster fish in a miniature puddle.

The district attorney said, "He'll give me more. When my support starts rolling in."

She hoped that that support never materialized. She did not want her husband to run for governor. Several times, at length, they had discussed what the wear and tear from the campaign could do to him, but he had his mind set on the high office. "Take the money back," she said, "and throw it in his face."

"What would that solve?"

"It would tell him you're not a menial. He's beholden."

"He's beholden only as much as he wants to be. I should have realized it would be that way."

"Now you know."

"Yes," he said. "Now I know."

She watched him scratch out his cigarette, only the filter left, and reach for another, stretching the tendons in his neck. She got up, a small figure of a woman whose recipe for pot roast was printed last year in *Yankee* magazine.

"Chugger," she said. "You look tired. Let's go to bed."

"He saw me," Officer Leo Morin said from beneath his oversized cap. "He knew it was me."

"So what?"

"I never should've done what you asked."

"Too late now."

The two officers faced each other over the hot hood of a cruiser. The left side of Sergeant Wilbur Cox's face was swollen and discolored, raw where the skin was perforated. He spoke from the right side of his jaw.

"If I wanted to I could bring charges against him, intent to commit murder."

"Why don't you then?"

"It's between him and me. He sits down at his desk he smells me. He knows I'm going to be sitting there one of these days. You'd better know it too."

Officer Morin yanked open the cruiser door and ducked in behind the wheel, dislodging his cap. It fell in his lap like a wounded bird. "I don't feel so hot. I'm going home."

Sergeant Cox peered in from the other window, his mouth rupturing into a threatening smile. "Make a choice kid. You want to be a real cop, or his kind, which is a joke?"

"Neither," Leo Morin said and sped off, burning rubber, as if he feared being fired upon.

Chief Jenkins drove through the dusk to Ed Robertshaw's house on Strawberry Drive. One of the sisters answered his ring. Ed Robertshaw was somewhere on the grounds, or at least he was the last she knew. "I'll find him," the chief said and found him near the static of an electric bug-killer, noisy executions, which they moved away from to better hear themselves. They faced each other near ornamental evergreens barbered into cubes and cones. Ed Robertshaw was not pleased to see him.

"I don't do business at home. If you have something to discuss, you make an appointment. Then we'll talk at the shack."

"You do business with the district attorney here," the chief said, and Ed Robertshaw looked at him with begrudging respect.

"You don't miss much. I must've known that when I made you chief. What do you want, Paul?"

"I've got thirty-six gun applications on my desk."

"I don't mind people being armed. It's the American way."

"Bingham Hardware has run out of locks. The Mitchells have canceled their lobster bake, first time in twenty years. Nobody trusts anybody else, and nobody buys the story about a shark. Instead they pair Lyman's death with the dentist's, a logical thing to do, since they were two of a kind. And nobody believes Bud Brown's a killer, when Bud's almost dead himself now. 'Who's going to be next?' That's what they're asking."

"Look up," Ed Robertshaw commanded quietly, and his arm arched high. "Look way up," he said, pointing to the roof of his grand house. "You want to talk about victims? There's a victim."

Craning his neck, the chief glimpsed a still figure, thin and wraithlike, grooved into the pinkish gray sky. It was Amy Robertshaw perched on the widow's walk, though for a moment the chief thought it was the ghost of his wife in the muted play of light. He said nothing.

Ed Robertshaw said, "I love my daughter, do you doubt that? Do you even understand it? At night my sisters see her holding her wrists up to the light, looking at the veins. She doesn't want to be part of this world anymore. That's why she's up there. Pretty soon I'll have to go up and bring her down, maybe even carry her, and my sisters will put her to bed." He smiled up at her through the distance. "You can't tell from here, or maybe you can, look at her, she's an old woman. Mental cruelty's a tame term for what she went through married to Lyman Arnold. He took all the spirit and self-respect out of her and he crushed something sweet and precious. That's what he left."

The chief dropped his eyes.

"You and me, Paul, we try to protect our women, not always intelligently, but we try."

"As you say, not always intelligently."

"Everybody cuts corners, Paul. Everybody does for his own. In business and politics I may be a son of a bitch, that's my way, but basically I'm a decent human being same as you. No?"

"I don't know what I am. All I know is I'm worried. From the start there've been too many side effects. Too many people touched. I can't keep my eye on everybody."

"Maybe you worry too much."

"I love this town," the chief said with passion. "I don't want to see it come apart."

Winnie Wallace and Pamela Comeau met on the boulevard, perhaps by chance, it seemed that way, and then they began walking together. The odd thing was that they did not talk, not until they left the boulevard and ventured up Strawberry Drive where maples and oaks shone as if from varnish against the low light of the sky. "Do you know whose house that is?" Winnie asked. They stood across from it. They were shadows between trees, sharp faces beneath the branches. Winnie, her bust tightly bound, wore a strapless top and straight trousers. Pamela, in sweatshirt and jeans, looked like a schoolgirl beside her.

"How would I know?"

"It's historic. The first Robertshaw here was a Canuck named Robichaud, from Prince Edward Island, the Puerto

Rican of his time. He built the house. He was a rumrunner and a fence. Pirates rowed in with loot from their ships. That's the reason for the widow's walk. So he could see their signal. Also so he could watch over the whole town. He felt it was his. He changed his name and became a Yankee."

"The widow's walk. Somebody's up there." Pamela spoke tentatively, for the distant figure atop the massive house seemed dimensionless, an intermittent flash as if off glass dulled by the ravages of weather. "Who is it?"

"You don't know, do you?" Winnie said and then quietly told her.

"Why did you bring me here?" Pamela asked with a shudder.

"It was an accident. I wasn't looking where we were going."

They went on the alert as a car rumbled down the Robertshaw driveway. It was a Ford, unmistakably the police chief's, and they each pulled back. The Ford rattled onto the street. Apparently without seeing them, the chief drove away.

The color of the sky altered rapidly. Now it was mauve, creating an impression of mildew and dust. Visible only in intervals, the figure in the widow's walk wavered as though touched by a stray current of air. Pamela tensed.

"Is she safe up there?"

"Will she jump? Will the wind take her away? I don't know." Winnie smiled obliquely. "I don't know about myself anymore."

"Can she fend for herself?"

"Not like us."

"I'd like to talk to her."

There was a gentle shake of the head. "She wouldn't understand, or want to."

"We're all widows," Pamela murmured. "Maybe I could tell her that."

Fiercely nearsighted, Amy Robertshaw could not possibly have seen the two women shadowed beneath the trees, but Pamela felt that in some unaccountable way the message had got through and gazed over her shoulder as Winnie guided her away.

It was dusk by the time they made their way back to the boulevard. Joan and Laura were on the far side, their faces anxious. Their eyes fastened on Winnie, who said, "I don't think they know what to make of me. That's all right. Neither do you."

Pamela looked toward the traffic. "I know I can trust you."

"Yes," Winnie said. "Yes, you can."

Her stomach had bothered her, and twice she had all but thrown up. Now, feeling only slightly better, she drank weak tea and made a telephone call. She was confused when a child with a grownup voice finally answered the ring. "Who is this?" she asked through a cramp.

"Laurie."

"You the oldest?"

"Yes."

"What took you so long to answer?"

"I'm making supper."

"That's your mother's job. Not yours."

"I help. Do you want to speak to her?"

"No," Cora Dray said. "Put your father on."

Alice Cross, who as usual had lingered at the station long after Bess Cook had relieved her, edged uncertainly around the chief's desk. His head was bowed, and she could not see his eyes. He was surrounded by a quiet she was reluctant to break. She whispered, "Bess is afraid to drive home alone tonight when she gets off her shift."

"I'll drive her," the chief mumbled.

"No, it's okay. I've made arrangements."

"Then why did you bother me about it?"

"Don't be short," she said and watched him raise his head. He looked done in, afloat, as if no longer linked to his past, which frightened her. The past, she felt, was her only real grip on him. "Do you know what hurts me, Paul? You've stopped confiding in me."

He only half heard her. Squint-eyed, fingers laced together, he sat pitched at his desk like a motorist waiting for the green glow. A thumb twitched.

"Too much on your shoulders," she said in a propitiating tone. "You need things to be normal again."

This time, deep in thought, he did not hear her at all.

"I know your problems, Paul. You're a lonely guy. My daughter never should have died. You never should have been left alone."

"Alice."

"What, Paul?" She moved close and dropped a hand on his shoulder.

"Go home," he said. "Please."

A crease ran down a page of the *Times*, through the crossword puzzle, impossible to smooth, but Laura Kimball kept trying. To hide her anxiety, she whistled Chopin. Joan Weiss uncorked a bottle of wine and took a breath before pouring any.

"If she had told us where she was going, we wouldn't have worried."

Laura was more realistic. "Yes, we would have."

"Not as much."

"Yes, as much. Or more."

It was nine o'clock. Joan took a sip and peered through a screen window. The beach was dark. "Where is she now?"

"Jogging along the surf."

Joan was shocked. "She *can't be.*"

"She feels it's her right."

"That's not the point."

"She's not slipping back into a shell. At least that's something."

"But we can't watch her every minute."

"We can try," Laura said and abandoned the *Times.* Her dark eyes were resigned, and her long intelligent face was composed. The wine was too warm for Joan, and she carried the bottle into the pantry and opened the refrigerator. For a number of moments she stood in the sheet of cold that floated out.

"How much do you think she's told Winnie about herself?"

"I don't know," Laura said from the table. "I can't ask her. I'm not even sure what the relationship is. Nothing surprises me anymore."

The telephone rang from the wall. Tuned low, it let out only a muted jingle, but both women gave a start. Laura answered it, pushing back her dark hair to accommodate the receiver. Joan strode swiftly to her side. There was static on the line, and Laura said, "I'm sorry, but you'll have to speak up." A second later she wrapped a quick hand over the mouthpiece. "I think it's the police chief."

Joan tried to show no emotion but could not prevent a quaver in her voice. "Is it about Pam?"

"I don't know." Laura loosened her fingers. "What do you want?"

Joan pressed nearer with mounting apprehension and

slanted her head in a vain effort to catch the chief's voice. At the same time she tried to censor her thoughts.

"Take it," Laura said and abruptly thrust the phone at her. She took a dizzy step away from it. Laura said, "Are you free for dinner tomorrow? He wants to know."

There was a look of incredulity. "Tell him no."

"Tell him yes," Laura urged.

At that moment Pamela appeared in the doorway, her step sprightly, her sweatshirt damp, and her eyes audacious and dauntless. Her gaze went from one friend to the other.

Joan said, "Tell him maybe."

Sixteen

In the night Sergeant Wilbur Cox removed his pants, and all his change fell out, clattering on the carpetless floor. His wife, tensely awake, feigned sleep until he put rough hands on her. It was a brutal coupling, not a word said, not even when he hurt her, which he went out of his way to do. She pretended to enjoy.

In the morning he was up before she, which was unusual. She heard him in the bathroom. He showered for an inordinately long time. She feared staying in bed, and she feared leaving it. Mostly she feared thinking. After slipping on a limp robe, the goodness long ago laundered out of it, she retrieved coins from the floor and dutifully placed them on his bureau, though for a moment or so she kept two in her hand, a Kennedy half-dollar and a Roosevelt dime, as if she might take them and run.

He had left the bathroom a mess. She flushed the john and cleaned the sink with a towel he had discarded. With a hand flattened over her mouth, she stared in the mirror and tried not to cry. Her dread had grown, reaching her vitals. She showered for nearly as long as her husband had.

He was not in the kitchen. She called his name and then saw that his cap was gone. Her relief was immense, letting her enjoy the washed smells of morning that poured through the open window over the sink. The septic smell from the back yard would come later, with the heat. She was pouring coffee when her daughter Laurie, wearing pajamas too small for her, made a quiet entrance. "Daddy's still home," the child whispered.

Gladys Cox froze.

Wilbur Cox appeared in the next instant. He was in full uniform and viewed her from under the visor of his squared cap, stone chips for eyes.

Gladys managed a voice. "I thought you'd left."

He said, "Why didn't you ask me what that call I got last night was all about?"

"I thought if it was anything important you'd have told me."

"That's right. It wasn't anything important."

She shrank back. "Why are you looking at me that way?"

"Guess."

She wished her life were over. She would have signed her own death certificate on the dotted line and attached a picture, the pretty one of her from her high school yearbook. *The loveliest manners and the sweetest heart.* Those were the words printed beneath the picture.

"You bitch," her husband said almost under his breath, his smile chilling, and she knew what was coming.

"Please. Not in front of Laurie."

He pushed her toward the basement door. "Open it," he said, and she did, clicking on the light. "Go ahead," he said with another push. Her eyes were closed, her expression caught up in an air of fatality. She knew the stairs by heart. She was halfway down when he kicked her.

At a point near the Coral Motel a boy of four or five, fat and bespectacled, ventured into the water and let it lap at his round knees. His mother called him back. She was afraid of sharks.

"You don't have to worry," said Chief Jenkins, who had

stopped to watch. He knew from her accent that she was from New York or New Jersey. "No sharks around here," he said.

"A man was killed by one."

"Nobody's anywhere near sure of that."

The woman, wiry and springy, spun her son up into her arms. "Nobody's anywhere near sure of anything in this town."

The chief, who felt he had a case to make, said, "Nobody else is staying out of the water."

"That's their business," she said and carried the boy away.

The chief plodded on, a good quarter of a mile, dropping deep prints into the sand. Small shore birds skittered over a wide bed of pebbles. The ocean was expanding, coming in. The chief loosened his shirt from his chinos and rolled up the sleeves. In the distance he saw a number of children and a couple of adults gathered around something. Thinking that somebody was hurt, he ran toward them.

He pulled up short and more than slightly winded when he smelled what they were looking at. He threaded his way through the children, and the two adults made room for him. The carcass of a fish had washed up, too rank for the chief. He instantly backed off. It was a sand shark, scarcely two feet long and dead as if from having bitten something bad.

Cora Dray stepped out of her house. The grass spoke of her husband's absence. It needed cutting. She would have to hire a boy to do the job, one of the Farnhams, which did not please her.

She was no longer sure about the rose bushes. Perhaps she would let them grow wild to match her own new set of feelings. She glanced toward the garage where her husband's Cadillac was stored. She would have to do something about that and decided she would rely on Skelly to sell it for her. The

Corvette would be hers. She knew her brother would never use it again. As she walked toward it in the drive, she saw a figure on the sidewalk. Her eyebrows shot up. "What do you want?"

The minister's wife had trouble speaking. Drained of color, she took a weak step forward. "You have the right to hurt me," she said, "but why my husband?"

"Why not him?" Cora said with deadly nonchalance. "Why not everybody?"

"Have you become evil?"

"Yes, evil. If you want to think that."

"What else am I to think?"

"Think what you want," Cora Dray said quietly and surely, as if working from a glorious advantage. "By the way, where'd you get the face job? I might try one myself."

"Cora." The minister's wife trembled. "I've told him everything."

"Yes. I figured you would."

"He's forgiven me."

"Of course," Cora Dray said blithely. "But he'll never forget."

"You're right. He never will."

"Neither will I."

Pamela Comeau placed a call to Seattle and spoke to her former husband, who was polite but aloof, as if she were a stray fact in his past that no longer needed to be acknowledged. She wanted to speak to her children, but he said, "Do you ever hear from that guy?"

The question was cruel but expected. "Never, John. He's gone. He's gone forever." Her voice was hollow. "May I speak to my daughter? Please."

"Why do you keep doing this to yourself?" He was trying

to be kind. "You only upset her and hurt yourself."

"Will she talk with me?"

"You know the answer to that. Pam, give her time."

"Yes." She spoke through a commotion of feelings. "Time. And by then she'll be grown up. I won't know her."

"Do you know her now? I sure don't. She's not the same girl anymore."

"Nobody's the same anymore, John. I'm not either." She spoke starkly while twisting the telephone cord around her wrist. She wanted to scream out at him and the world, but she restrained herself. "May I speak to John Junior?"

"I'm sorry, Pam. He feels the same way."

The discussion was dead, and she held the phone down by her side long after he had disconnected.

"I'm all right, dear. Don't you worry." Gladys Cox's voice bloated because she had put a tooth through her upper lip, which had doubled in size. Her left eye was discolored and closed. She lay where her husband had thrown her, against unwashed clothes in the laundry room. Laurie stroked her hand.

"Mommy, can you move?"

She couldn't. Ribs were broken, which was the reason she was taking short breaths, and her back was sprained. It was her back that hurt the most.

"Mommy, tell me what to do."

"Is he gone?"

"Yes," Laurie said, as if having risen in size and strength she had driven her father out of the house.

"A blanket, dear. I'm cold."

There was a blanket on the bed down there in the basement, but instead Laurie raced upstairs, where the younger children immediately clustered around her, making her the mother. The face of the youngest boy was juicy with tears. "Everybody be quiet!" she ordered and grabbed for the telephone.

A few minutes later she was back down in the laundry room shaking out a quilt. The swollen weight of it disturbed Gladys, but the warmth was welcomed.

"Mommy, I called an ambulance."

"Why dear? Why'd you do that?"

The child could no longer hold back tears.

"It's all right," Gladys rasped. "I'll tell you a story while we wait. Once upon a time—"

"Mommy, don't. I'm too old."

As if touched by unseen fingers, Pamela Comeau flinched. Someone's eyes were on her. She stood austere and puritanical, select and private, near a stretch of shore where the swimming was bad, too many rocks. She was as far from the crowd as she could manage but never, it seemed, far enough. A man smoking a perfecto and wearing a print shirt circled her and then wandered off. Imperceptibly she relaxed a little and through dark glasses watched a boy throw bits of bread and draw gulls from every direction. A voice cut through her concentration.

"Hello there."

Unprepared for company, she stood as a straight line in her sleeveless robe. She could have been silk or steel. Her bathing suit was wet beneath the robe, for she had been in the water, where the rocks were. Her blond hair had dried flat, full of salt, which was also on her lips. She did not move.

"I thought it was you." Winnie Wallace glided over the sand in flat shoes and cream colors, her graying curls dazzling in the sun. A smile slipped forth. "You're easy to spot."

"Were you looking for me?"

"In a way. I was worried."

"Why?" Pamela asked with a sharp glance.

"Can't I worry if I want?"

"I wish you wouldn't."

"I'm sorry." Winnie flushed. "I presume too much."

A silence developed as people traipsed by, sun-struck figures, and both women were conscious of shivers of heat, parched skin, fever blisters. Two boys in tiger-striped trunks copied their father's stride. A pack of adolescent girls ranged by, comfortable with their youth and beauty, followed by their mothers, goddesses gone fat.

Winnie said, "I've been at the Smiths, remember them? They were at your party. They want me to sublet their cottage for the rest of the season, which won't be easy for obvious reasons."

Pamela bent her head to cough, a nervous noise, too much smiting her senses. She had no clear recollection of the Smiths or even of the party.

"That night in your room," Winnie said after a painful hesitation. "I've never analyzed it."

"Nor do you need to."

"I haven't even wondered if it could happen again."

"It couldn't."

"It could," Winnie said nakedly, "but it won't. I understand that perfectly."

Pamela had no comment, and Winnie was all of a sudden embarrassed, rosy in the face and redder in the neck. She had sunglasses somewhere. Ferreting in her bag, she found them and put them on. The lenses were smudged.

"I talk too much, I know. My problem is I'm not sure of myself, never have been. I have to invent myself each day. You know, a fresh face. This morning, for instance, I looked in the mirror and saw somebody I almost liked for a change.

That's a great feeling. I feel great right this minute."

"I'm glad for you."

"Maybe it will last."

"Nothing lasts, you can be sure of that."

There was another hesitation from Winnie, though less painful, almost joyful in a way. "Women should stick together. Being self-centered, I never used to think that way, but I've come around."

Pamela's face tightened to the bone. The man smoking the perfecto had returned, worse for the wear, sapped by the sun. Pamela had the illusion that she could smell his cigar breath coming out of his cooked mouth. His manner was inquisitorial, and his eyes strafed her.

"Why?" she murmured. "Why do I attract them? Do I look that easy?"

"Him?" Winnie whipped off her dark glasses, and in the glare her eyes seemed too vulnerable a blue to see anything. "You mean him?" She moved forward a step. "You're not easy. You just don't know how to make them go away."

The man, a good thirty feet away, had a big voice, the kind meant to bowl people over. "Excuse me," he said, and Winnie, slow and deliberate, pivoted in his direction.

"Piss off!" she said.

His breath blew hard as he plodded over the sand, a sweating bull of a man with much neck flesh. His print shirt lay plastered against his deep chest, and his seersucker trousers pulled at the knee with each belabored step. Chucking away the stub of the perfecto, he gazed over shelves of sand at the gray house, its porch, its shingles. The hanging fuchsia looked like a fist of fire. Twice before he had climbed the high porch steps, each time finding no one home. He had left his business card in the screen door and his rental car on the bou-

levard, bugs beaten into the windshield. He had come a long
way, Air Florida to Boston and Hertz to here. Consulting his
digital gold watch, he decided to give the porch a third try.

His card was gone from the screen. The door squalled
open.

"What do you want?"

Joan had the card in her fingers. Her wheat hair fell long
and the cool color of her beach dress contrasted sharply with
her hot tan. She blocked his way by twisting her weight forward on one leg, the calf handsome, a perfect shape.

Louis Weiss slid her a sly look and whispered, "Jesus, you
look good."

Seventeen

Fastened into the crowd at the state liquor store on Route One were fiercely altered faces of people Chief Jenkins had known from childhood. Most were stocking up for the weekend. When the chief approached, they shied away with untrusting looks and half-nods. A dour woman in a mesh-weave jersey, a forbidden sweet in high school, openly snubbed him, but her husband, whose glossy hairpiece fooled no one, paused thoughtfully. When the chief weeded his way to a counter to write out his order, the husband followed. He had been a teammate of the chief's, basketball. In fact, he had been the captain. He whispered, "We expected better from you, Paul."

Poising a pencil, the chief stared up at the taller man, whose long face was unfinished at the chin. Except around the middle, he was still thin, a spike. "What are you talking about, Jimmy?"

"You know."

The chief played dumb. Jimmy was a salesman, sporting goods, New Hampshire and Vermont and parts of Maine, his life estimated in car miles. He assumed a hard, determined stance, as though placing himself back on the basketball court. The team had never been outstanding, only lively.

"People don't like being lied to," he said. "And they don't like being scared. My wife never minded being alone when I took my trips. Now she does. I make good money doing what I do. I don't want to change that."

The chief sympathized with his eyes.

"We've got a right to know who bashed in Bud Brown. That would go a long way towards easing our minds, because then we could probably figure out for ourselves who's really been doing these killings. You see what I'm saying, Paul? If we got less bullshit and more truth, we wouldn't have to wonder and worry."

The chief was quiet.

"And the wife would sleep better."

He was also deadpan. He still held the pencil. It was just a stub, chewed at the top, but the point was pristine. He stared at the order blank.

"Don't you have anything to say?"

"I'm trying to think of something."

Jimmy gentled his tone, somewhat. "People don't feel they can trust you anymore. Some figure you're covering for a friend. Others guess you've got Ed Robertshaw on your back. Maybe you're beholden to him, Paul, but not when it comes to murder. His son-in-law died funny. You know it, and I know it. Everybody does."

The chief gazed into the crowd's hot variety of faces. He appeared to smile.

"What's funny?"

"I've learned to laugh. I don't laugh loud, you understand, but I've learned to laugh."

"What's that supposed to mean?"

"I don't know."

"You should play straight, Paul. Don't go for the hard shot when you've got an easy one. I remember the night we lost to Exeter. You were playing cute. That's how come you pulled your knee apart."

"I remember."

"I think you were showing off for Winnie Wallace."

"I probably was."

"No bra under her sweater. Remember that?"

"I do, Jimmy."

"You were the one who scored with her, we didn't."

"I had to score at something as I remember."

Jimmy assumed a sober air, bringing himself partly back to the present. "Your job, I guess it isn't easy."

"Usually a piece of cake, Jimmy, but lately a challenge."

"Even if you don't win, at least look good. That's what the coach used to tell us."

"I can hear his voice," the chief said and began scribbling on the order blank. Jimmy's wife came near, diffusing the same scent she'd worn in high school. Blue Grass. Her voice was stiff.

"I didn't know you were a drinker, Paul."

His eyes slid forward to meet hers. She had a somber way of smiling. The chief said, "I like a little wine in the house."

"How's Winnie?" she said with the remoteness of lost years, all of them unretrievable, even with the Blue Grass. "I imagine you see her once in a while."

"Yes. Once in a while."

He purchased the wine and left.

Louis Weiss, his print shirt open to below the chest, sat frowning from a wicker chair. He was a bourbon-drinker, but Joan had only chilled wine to give him. Eyeing the stemmed glass in her hand, he said, "Let's go out somewhere, that might be better."

"No. Do you want this or not?"

"I'll take it." His hand was huge, the nails manicured. He drank the wine with thirst if not enjoyment. When Joan asked whether he wanted more, he said, "I'll wait." She sat across from him in an identical chair, her knees jammed together. They spoke of their son. "Is he still on drugs?" he asked.

"He smokes pot. Who doesn't?"

"I don't. You don't."

"How do you know what I do, Louis?"

"You're right. I don't." He was edgy, restless. He needed another cigar, but he had no more, which, he told himself, was just as well. He heard the hum of voices from an adjoining room. "Can't say I like your friends."

"You don't have to."

"The blonde. She's spooky."

"Just leave her alone, Louis."

"Are you kidding? I wouldn't go near her." His voice became whisper-soft. "I've missed you, Joanie."

She pretended not to hear. She said, "How have you been?"

"I could be a lot better." He'd had a coronary, a small one, but he feared the possibility of a far worse one. "She doesn't look after me the way you did," he said, referring to the young woman once his secretary and now his wife.

"What can I say, Louis?"

"No sympathy?"

"Of course. Some."

"Sometimes I wake up at three in the morning and can't get back to sleep. I hate it when it happens. I start thinking about you."

"Take a pill."

"I take enough of those."

She smiled dimly. He had never been cruel, simply selfish and unfaithful. She knew his visit here was only incidental in his trip up from Palm Beach. He still had properties in and around Boston that needed attention. He was a landlord, a developer, a speculator, and, when he had the time, a practicing lawyer. He stared at her with expressive eyes.

"There was a guy you were seeing, I forget his name."

"That was a long time ago."

"You're not seeing him anymore?"

"No."

"Are you celibate or something?"

"None of your business."

A number of mute moments passed. Louis Weiss slanted his head and touched his hair where it was going thin. Planted in the chair, he assumed a weary anonymity, which was lately a trick of his, a ruse for sympathy. "This is a big house," he observed. "You must have an extra room."

"I know what you're asking, and the answer's no."

"Christ, I'm tired. I'm not the bruiser I used to be."

"Louis, don't."

He looked hurt. "Where's your hospitality, Joanie?"

"Squeeze harder," Winnie Wallace said, wincing. "Squeeze with all your might." Cora Dray had come up from behind and grabbed her wrist. They were in the rear of Philpott's. Other customers were all at the front of the store, at the snack bar and near the cash register. "That the best you can do?" There were tears of pain in Winnie's blue eyes but a small triumphant smile on her lips. "I think you've shot your load."

Cora gradually released her grip while holding her ground. She'd been drinking sherry at home, quite a bit, and was staying afloat through sheer will power. Her nostrils flared.

"Sober, you might've broken it," Winnie said, rubbing her wrist. Nearby was a door with a No Entry sign. It led to a storeroom. Cora seemed to nod at it. "No," said Winnie. "Say what you've got to say here. If you want the town to hear, holler it."

Cora poked her jaw forward while trying to gather a voice, not necessarily a loud one. Her mouth was open.

"Do you want to call me a slut?" Winnie asked. "Go ahead. I can take that. Do you want to know if I killed your husband? I didn't. I can scratch and bite and spit, but I don't know anything about shooting a gun. That's the God's honest truth, Cora, so help me."

There was a flurry at the front of the store, children galloping in, a rush to the snack bar, ice cream wanted. A mother shouted to two of the children, their names ricocheting down an aisle.

Winnie said, "I wish I had a Bible, I'd slap my hand on it."

Cora's voice came out wrong. It was tiny and thin and sounded like an old man's. "Did you talk about me?"

"Not a word. You know how he was. He talked about himself. Sometimes, when I could get him to listen, I talked about me. That was a coup."

"I can crush you." The voice was hoarse. "I can find ways."

"I don't doubt it for a second. I'm not as tough as I sound. I'm not even half as tough as I sound. You should see me sometimes when I'm all alone. A real crybaby."

"Do you think he loved you? I can tell you he didn't."

"He never said he did, so I imagine you're right."

"Did you love him?"

"Jesus Christ, Cora, what's love? Some man's fingers in the crack of your ass? If you've got a nicer answer, tell me, I'm anxious to know."

"You have all the right quips, don't you?" Cora said from a parched throat. Lips squirming, she struggled for moisture and mustered more than she'd hoped for. She spat in the other's face. Then she slapped it, bumping against children too fascinated to move. A sudden jolt of insight brought her up short, and her seeing eye flashed with hate.

Winnie smiled obscurely behind the spit and the sting, as if she'd been anointed and blessed. Absolved.

★ ★ ★ ★ ★

Joan came down the stairs and, opening a closet to the smell of naphthalene, drew clean white sheets from one shelf and towels from another. A voice seemingly pushed at her from nowhere. "Will he be staying long?"

"The night. That's all."

Pamela broke from a web of shadows where shades had been lowered against the late sun and stood almond-eyed like a cat gently retracting its claws. She had on a shapeless sweatshirt and shorts. The blue bruise showed on her shin. Her face was smooth, hard, and beautiful. "What's he doing now?"

"He brought a suitcase in from his car. He wants to take a shower."

"He isn't what I pictured."

Joan closed the closet and draped the sheets and towels over one arm. "He's not a brute, Pam. And he wasn't trying to pick you up on the beach. He was looking for me, asking around."

"I understand that now," Pamela said without conviction.

"I can still tell him to go."

"No. I can manage."

Joan moved closer, calculating in her mind the dangers, risks, and liabilities. "Pam, I wouldn't want anything bad to happen."

"You mustn't worry. I can function. I'm not an emotional cripple."

Quietly, Laura joined them, carrying copies of the *Boston Globe* and *New York Times* under one arm. She'd read parts of them in the morning and meant to finish up now. She'd been out on the porch for a strong sniff of salt air. "Is there a problem?" she asked.

Joan shot a glance at Pamela, who said, "I wish people wouldn't worry about me."

★ ★ ★ ★ ★

Joan saw him as he came out of the bathroom, parts of him still wet, a towel matted around his beefy neck. He was clad only in drooping underpants. "Your best behavior, Louis. I need your promise."

"You've got it," he said with a persuasive smile. Despite his gut, he was not an unattractive man.

"And please don't go around like that."

"I forget. This isn't my house."

"It's not mine either. I share it. Remember that too."

"Yes, ma'am."

He went into the room she'd assigned him, and she slipped into hers, closing the door. It was later than she'd thought, six-thirty, and she needed to shower, do something with her face, and decide on a dress. She stripped quickly and got into a robe, then wasted time near a window, for she enjoyed gazing at the ocean. She did not hear him come in, though perhaps she should've expected it, along with what happened next. He crept up behind her and, sliding his hands beneath her arms, parted the robe and caressed the naked front of her. His breath went down the back of her neck. His aftershave was cloying.

"How have you been, darling?"

"Louis, this is not going to work," she said, cold to his touch. "Honest, it isn't."

"I still think of you as my wife."

"You ought not to. You have a very pretty one in Florida. You should have brought her with you, Louis, and we could have avoided this."

"Joanie, I've been dying to do this." His busy hands indulged themselves. His fingers were charged, increasingly insistent.

"That doesn't do anything to me, Louis. I'm sorry."

Moving, she accidentally bumped his mouth as he tried to kiss the top of her head. She broke from him, securing her robe, and fended off his attempt to reconnect. He looked doleful and disappointed but not surprised.

"You must feel something for me." He suddenly looked jowly and old. "You kept my name."

"Of course I feel something for you," she said, in no way wishing to hurt him but with no reserve of energy to deal with him. "That has nothing to do with keeping your name. It would have been too much of a chore to change it. Besides, I'm used to it."

"Don't shut me out entirely," he said, now with a certain timidity. "Let me take you out to dinner."

"That's not possible, Louis. I'm sorry."

"Why isn't it possible?"

"I'm having dinner with someone else."

"Who?"

She smiled faintly, not confident that he would believe her. "The police chief," she said.

Eighteen

"You're struggling to be civil."

"I don't mean to give that impression."

"But you feel forced into being here with me."

"A little."

Chief Jenkins changed the subject by screwing his eyes into the wine menu. "I don't know any of these names. Or even how to pronounce them."

"Would you like me to order?"

"Please."

Joan asked for a half-bottle of *Graves Blanc*, her loose brown hair trembling as she spoke. The chief had primped for the occasion, having chosen a delicately dotted tie to go with his button-down shirt and soft summer-weight suit. The only incongruity was his desert boots, which he kept hidden under the table. The dining room of the Exeter Inn had a tranquil air of elegance. The flowers were fresh, the linen dazzling. The chief hesitated loosening his napkin. There were no more than a dozen other patrons, most of whom looked like elderly alumni of Phillips Exeter Academy.

The chief said, "Why only a half-bottle?"

"You're driving. And I don't quite trust your car."

"One of the tires is low. I keep shoving air into it, but it keeps coming down."

"I'm sure there's a remedy."

They had strawberry soup for an appetizer. It tasted like a milk shake to the chief, who wished the serving had been

172

larger. The wine arrived with dinner, which came on a cart. They had ordered sole and in silence watched the waitress bone it. When they began eating, the chief said, "Why do I have the feeling you've been here before?"

"My son went to the academy."

"I should have guessed."

"Why should you have guessed? Why should you guess anything about me?" She squirted lemon on her sole. "Why am I of interest to you?"

"You're a woman."

"And you're a man. All right, Chief, I'll leave it at that."

He forked up a dollop of potato. He could have done without the cheese on it. "Who's the fellow at your place?"

"My former husband. Do we need to discuss him?"

"No, not at all."

"I suspect a question will hang. For years the marriage was bad, but the divorce was amicable. He just happened to stop by and will be gone tomorrow."

"My wife died years ago."

"I'm sorry to hear that." Soft piano music could be heard. The player was concealed behind potted fig trees. "I suppose the next question is why you never married again."

"Sometimes I wish I had. It's not too late, I guess, though I kind of think it is for me. I seem to be married to my job."

"Do you like it that much, your job?"

"Sometimes I just need somebody to talk it over with."

Joan Weiss stiffened slightly and gave a secret look at her watch. The look was not secret enough. "I'm sorry," she said. "That was rude of me."

"How's your sole?"

"It's lovely," she said. She'd eaten as much as she could. The chief had finished his. He poured more wine, both glasses, finishing the bottle. The piano player was rendering another tune.

"Perry Como used to sing that."

"Vaguely I remember. He also cut hair."

"Yes, he did."

"Are you in a mood, Chief?"

"A bit of one." He picked up his wine glass. "Tell me about your parents."

"Good God. Are you really interested or simply being polite? My father lives in Florida and my mother's dead. She died hard. Cancer."

"I didn't mean to stir up bad memories." He was abashed. "I'm sorry."

"It's okay. I don't think about death. I can't picture myself as a skeleton."

"Neither can I. How about dessert?"

She did not want any. While he ordered coffee, she gave another secret look at her watch, this time without his noticing. While they waited for the coffee, he spoke of the weather, the stretch of ideal beach days. The previous summer had been wetter, downright miserable at times. She had no comment. He shifted the conversation to crime, the relative lack of it in Boar's Bluff until this season. "Then, boom, everything happens at once," he said, quickly mentioning the brutal beating of Bud Brown and the homicide of Stephen Dray. Almost as an afterthought, he brought up the death of Lyman Arnold. "A few things on that one have not been made public," he confided.

The waitress served coffee, smiling at them. Joan did not touch her cup.

"People of course are upset," the chief went on. "Too many are buying guns." He paused. "Do you own one?"

"No," she said, looking beyond him.

"I thought you might, living in Cambridge, working in Boston."

"Mace, maybe. No gun."

"You have Mace?"

"I was joking." She gazed briefly into her coffee, then at him. "That's not to say I didn't consider getting one. There was a time I was afraid much of the time, after my divorce. I was afraid of subways, afraid of children who ran by me, of teenagers who hooted, of blacks who were polite to me. I was irrationally afraid of everything."

"I wouldn't have guessed that."

"It was sink or swim. I learned to float . . . then swim."

A silence rose up as their eyes disengaged. The chief toyed with his coffee cup and then lifted it. "Why so quiet?"

"I'm waiting for the other shoe to fall."

"What do you mean?"

She showed a shadowy smile. "I think you're playing Columbo."

"Be nice."

"Be honest." She shifted forward. "Why have you been so fired up to take me to dinner? I want to know why."

"Two reasons," the chief said. "I'm a lonely guy. My mother-in-law has stressed the point more than once."

"The other reason?"

"I'd like you to tell me what's wrong with Mrs. Comeau."

The doctor hovered small and fussy in front of the coffee machine and punched the button for black. Usually he was not at the hospital at this hour, but he had been attending a patient who had succumbed, an old man he had rather liked. Also he had looked in on a woman, a battered wife if he had ever seen one, but she had claimed otherwise, which had caused him to be short with her. He withdrew a steamy Styrofoam cup of coffee, which burnt his fingers. He shifted the cup to the other hand and then back again. A voice said, "Is that you?"

He turned around and was startled. He had thought the voice was a man's. Cora Dray came upon him with eyes beady and bloodshot, and instinctively the doctor's young face pulled in at the mouth. He suspected she was drunk. She smelled it.

"I want you to operate," she announced.

"We can't," he said in a monotone. "If we do, your brother will die."

"If you don't, he'll live dead."

The doctor did not hide his distaste. Many people annoyed him, but this woman more than most. He found her singularly overbearing. "We can't touch him. He's inoperable."

"Then why let him live?"

"I see. You'd rather he die."

"Is it my decision?"

"No. Thank God." The doctor was going to say more, but her eyes flattened out and burned on him. The silence was acute. She thrust herself closer, giving him more of her smell and the distinct impression that she had the power to annihilate him.

"Give me that," she said.

"What?" He was confused, off-balance.

"That!" she said and took the steaming coffee from his hand. "I need it more than you." As hot as the coffee was, she drained the cup. The doctor slipped away.

She made her way out of the hospital with steady and deliberate steps, the evening air still charged with the day's heat. The Corvette was parked next to a pickup truck, which shuddered. Skelly, with a struggle, climbed out of it. She had been waiting. Plunging her hands into her clean coveralls, she said, "Did you see him?"

Cora Dray nodded. "He looks sweet. Like a baby."

Skelly's full face pumped out a smile. "Does that mean he's getting better?"

"It only means he looks like a baby. Otherwise he's no different. He's never going to be any different."

Skelly peered up at the sky. "Is he hurting?"

Cora opened the door of the Corvette. "Maybe you should go see for yourself," she said after a calculated pause.

A car trundled by, an old model. The exhaust was overwhelming. Skelly passed a hand over her mouth. "Nobody should suffer."

Cora gave a vague nod. "Especially our Bud."

"Why?" she said. "Why are you so interested in Pam?"

"I'm interested in everybody in this town."

They had left the Exeter Inn and had driven back to Boar's Bluff. Now they were walking the beach, the chief's idea. The moon was soap-white, and the sand was salmon. More than once Joan gazed in the direction of the lighted gray house to reassure herself that all seemed serene. She said, "But you're singling her out."

"I told you. Her behavior struck me as strange. I thought she might need help."

"What are you accusing her of?"

"Nothing. What makes you think I am?"

"Please, don't turn my questions inside out. Back at the inn you said that everything hasn't been revealed about that Arnold man's death. Does that mean he was murdered?"

"I was talking out of school."

"I don't understand you."

"Look out," he said. In their path were the sea-soaked feathers and bones of a gull, the head gone. They veered to the left and for a short way followed the herringbone footprints of somebody's sneakers. The ocean was calm, all of a piece. The chief said, "I just thought Mrs. Comeau might have seen or heard something I should know."

"I doubt that." Joan stopped in her tracks and began slipping off her pumps. It was easier to walk without them. The chief stood still.

"She seems afraid of something."

"She's afraid of a lot of things. For God's sake, Chief, give her a break. The past few years haven't been good to her."

The chief was quiet for a long moment. "I'll back off if you like."

They began walking again. She carried her shoes dangling from one hand. The chief walked close to her. Despite the serenity of the ocean, they could feel the wrench of the waves, as if some of the waves were buried underfoot. She gave the chief a sideward glance and seemed to come to a small decision. She said, "Pam's a beautiful woman."

"Striking," the chief murmured.

"And all she ever wanted was a home and children. She has two children, both now at difficult ages, and she dearly misses them. They're clear across the country at present, with their father."

The chief spoke gently. "What happened to the marriage?"

"Her husband's company transferred him to Seattle, where, I understand, the rainy season got on his nerves, a situation he mitigated by having an affair. Then apparently he fell in love with the young woman. When it came time for Pam to join him out there, he didn't want her. Some wives handle that better than others. Pam was shattered. Then she did what many rejected women do. She plunged into a relationship with the first man who came along. He turned out to be a brute in a Brooks Brothers suit. If he hadn't split after a couple of months, I don't think anything would have been left of her. And there you have it, Chief. If Pam seems odd to you, there are reasons, which have nothing to do with you or anybody else in this town."

The chief's voice was subdued. "How is she now?"

"Better. Much better. We look after her."

"She's lucky to have friends like you and Mrs. Kimball."

"We do for each other."

The chief touched her forearm, almost a shy gesture. Then his hand slid regretfully away from her. "I like this," he said.

"What?"

"Walking with you."

She glanced at him, catching his profile in the marble light. Her shoes bumped against him.

"I like your company." His tone was mellow. He had an urge to speak about his wife, but he was quiet. There was always the danger of exalting her with false reminiscences. The problem was not that he had loved her a lot but that he had scarcely loved her at all. He had not been given the time.

Joan said, "Do you mind? I'm tired."

He walked her to the gray house, to the bottom step of the porch stairs, where window light slanted down on them. Her ear was tuned for sounds from the house, but there were none. The chief said, "I have a bottle of wine at my house. Nothing like what we had at the inn, but I was hoping we might share it. I guess not tonight."

"No, Chief, not tonight." She slipped on her shoes and viewed him noncommittally. "God, I wish I could read you."

Like a shy suitor, he kissed her cheek.

Something was wrong. Joan Weiss sensed it as soon as she stepped inside the house. Too many lights were on, but none was on in the front room, from which Laura Kimball emerged soundlessly, looking back once into the dark. Joan, heart fluttering, pitched forward.

"Tell me quick! What happened?"

"Pam was alone in her room," Laura said in a low voice, "brushing her hair. He crept in and put a hand on her shoulder."

"The idiot!"

"It's all right. She didn't do anything. I got there in time."

"Where is she now?"

"In there," Laura said with a gesture toward the darkness. "She's on the couch. I tried to make her take a pill, but she wouldn't. She dozed off anyway."

"Where's Louis?"

"Upstairs." Laura's long face was stark. Her voice, a cutting tool, edged into Joan. "You have to get him out of here. Either that or sleep with him to keep him safe."

Joan went up the stairway. The door to the room she had given him was closed. She entered without knocking. The light was on, and he was sitting up on the bed in his underpants. He had been reading newspapers, the *Globe* and *Times*, the sections scattered about. "Joan," he said, reaching out. He wanted her hand. He had hard lines in his forehead and a fluff of fat around his middle. "You know me well enough. I didn't mean anything. I didn't really even *do* anything."

"Louis. I want you to leave. Right now."

"Joanie, if you could have seen her eyes. I think she's got a screw missing."

"You shouldn't have touched her."

"It's you I want."

"Get out," she said, a vibration in her voice. "And don't come back."

When she returned downstairs, Laura was making coffee in the kitchen. The two stared at each other, and each thought the other looked haggard. Joan sat at the table.

"He'll be gone in five minutes."

Laura made no comment, but her shoulders noticeably relaxed, along with muscles in her neck, which she immediately kneaded. She joined Joan at the table.

"What does the police chief know?"

"If I knew the answer to that one," Joan said, "I'd sleep better tonight."

"What did you tell him about Pam?"

"Nothing he couldn't have dug up himself if he tried."

"Is he suspicious?"

"Yes," said Joan, "a little. And he wants me to know it."

Laura's reading glasses were on the table, and she put them on, black hornrims, which made her look prim and stern, more collected than she was, like the minister's wife she once was. She pushed back her dark hair. "Should we tell her?"

"In time we'll have to."

When the chief got home the telephone was ringing. His first inclination was to let it ring out. For a while it seemed he would, but then with a heavy arm he lifted the receiver. The caller was his mother-in-law. Alice Cross should not have been at the station at that hour, but that was where she was, her voice digging into his ear in a way her daughter's voice never had. She had been trying for two hours to reach him, her message urgent. The chief listened to it with only half a mind. He needed to use the bathroom and looked forward to it. He could read a whole magazine on the john.

"Did you hear what I said?"

"Something about Bud Brown."

"Damn it, Paul. Pay attention." Her voice shrilled, "He's dead!"

"Dead?"

"Someone ripped all the tubes out of him!"

Nineteen

Skelly sat on tires piled three high in an open bay of the Mobil station and watched the morning rain come down. She was ambivalent about rain, at times hating it and other times nursing memories she tried to make tender. In bygone days her whole family had bathed in the rain behind their unpainted shack, no plumbing, the children bouncing Ivory Soap around like a rubber ball while the father eyed daughters. She was the oldest. She could hear her mother's voice: "Leave 'em be, Ralph. Just leave 'em be."

Lightning irradiated Route One, branding cars. Thunder smashed, and the rain turned dramatic, draping the gasoline pumps and flooding the asphalt. Grease and oil spangled the rushing water. Skelly, in the dryness of the bay, lit a cigarette.

She remembered nights her father had lain on her for hours at a time while her mother worked the late shift, shucking clams. Then one night, before he had a chance to grab her, she smacked him with the tire iron she'd stolen from his junk car. Her mother nursed him back to physical health, but he turned simple, no memory of anything until the day he died, which wasn't so long ago.

She didn't want the cigarette and snapped it into the rain, but it blew back at her. She extended a foot and ground it out. For a long while she listened to the telephone ringing in the office. Finally it stopped, but then it started up again. The rain made the day dark, except when the lightning struck. A car banged through the downpour and swung wide into the lot, tires hissing as if boiling and the headlights flaring in a phantasmagoria of leaping shapes. The car stopped at the pumps and idled in place, its high beams glued to the rain. Skelly slid off the tires. Brushing the voluminous seat of her coveralls, she went into the office and answered the telephone.

"Do you hate me for it?" she said.

"I respect you." Cora Dray's voice came through dry as a bone. "You did what I couldn't."

"He's all right now. The dead don't feel anything."

There was a pause. "Are you scared, Skelly?"

Skelly's pause was longer. "Are you?"

"The nurses know he was alive when I left."

Skelly gazed down at her work shoes, steel-toed, the leather stained and nicked, and waited for the quiver in her lower lip to subside. Instead it worsened.

"You there?"

"Yes," Skelly said.

"A nurse remembered seeing somebody big leaving his room. She said it was a man. Maybe you don't have to worry."

The door flew open behind Skelly and rain blew in. "I gotta go," she said quickly and jammed the phone down, her other hand dropping over the handle of a wrench, which lay near the cash register. She shot a look over her shoulder and saw Chief Jenkins in the doorway, the rain pouring off his yellow slicker and puddles flashing at his feet. The hood of the slicker was over his head, framing his lean face, his mouth sadly crescent. Their eyes locked.

"Skelly."

The voice was so quiet she almost failed to hear it. She had hands like chunks of meat. One had a firm grip on the wrench, which she lifted surreptitiously and held down by her side. She waited for him to try to arrest her.

He said, "How about some gas?"

There were four beds in the room, and the chief, still wearing his slicker, went to the one where the curtain was partially drawn. He looked down at Gladys Cox, her face swelling up at him from the stark pillow. Her lips were black from being sutured. He said, "Can you speak?"

She nodded. There were no flowers on the bedside table, and he made a mental note to send her some. He touched her hand, which felt like a child's.

"I dropped in on you last night, but it was late. You were asleep." He paused for a second. "There was some excitement. Did you hear about Bud Brown?" She nodded and shuddered, and he could tell that she did not want to talk about it. But he wished to ease her mind. "Wilbur couldn't have done it. He was drinking at Peter's Place and was the last to leave. I checked."

"Thank you," she said in a small voice. "Thank you for telling me."

The chief again touched her hand, this time gently squeezing it. "You have internal injuries, Gladys. The doctor told me."

"Nothing serious."

"Serious enough. Will you sign a complaint?" He knew it was a foolish question, and he was sorry he had asked it. He leaned over and kissed her forehead. She turned her face to the wall.

"I don't want him to go to jail, Paul."

"I know."

"No, you don't. I want him to die."

Lieutenant Haas and the district attorney were drinking

Sanka in the hospital cafeteria. Chief Jenkins approached their table with a small glass of orange juice and joined them. He had met the district attorney on only a few brief occasions and was shocked to find him much gaunter and grayer than he remembered. He said, "How are you, sir?"

There was a nod, not much of one. The district attorney rubbed at the soreness in his fingers. He had been mingling with hospital personnel, pumping hands, politicking. He did not shake the chief's hand. Nor did Lieutenant Haas, whose scalp shone through his smooth hair.

The lieutenant said, "Did you get any sleep?"

"A little," the chief said, and the lieutenant brushed at his silk tie. The chief was beginning to know the gesture, along with the sniffing movement of the lieutenant's slim nose.

"What a mess. The Exeter police would rather not get involved. You can understand their position."

The chief said, "I wonder if they can understand mine."

"Naturally we want to clear this up as soon as possible. Anything you'd care to contribute we'd appreciate."

The district attorney, with the air of being totally out of the conversation, focused his attention on young nurses lining up with trays. He was not looking at them lasciviously, only admiringly, from the prop of an elbow. The chief, uncomfortable in his slicker, slipped it off and draped it over the back of his chair.

Lieutenant Haas said, "I don't know whether you've been told, but we're looking for a man. A big fellow. Fat. He might be some sort of maintenance worker or mechanic."

"What was he wearing?"

"The nurse wasn't sure. Overalls. Coveralls. She only saw him from the back. Sound like anybody you might know?"

The chief drank his juice, slowly. "Not offhand."

"My first thought was it might've been the guy who bashed him in."

"That was my first thought too."

"But you don't know who that is."

"No," the chief said quietly, aware that the district attorney was now looking at him. The district attorney drew in his elbows in an abstracted way.

"What's the mood in your town, Chief?"

"Suspicious, sir. Uneasy. People don't always swallow everything whole."

Lieutenant Haas said, "My second thought was that the sister might've hired the guy to put her brother out of his misery. I mean, she's weird, wouldn't you say?"

"I'd say," the chief offered slowly, "she loved her husband very much and her brother even more."

"How should I interpret that?"

"I don't know, Lieutenant. I'm not you."

The district attorney toyed with a pack of Benson & Hedges. "Are you a team player, Chief?"

"I used to be. But that was basketball."

The rain stopped at midday, and the sun came out, fierce rays that scorched puddles and heated the air. Joan walked with purpose near the white cottages, the sand jerking away underfoot. She was careful not to trample the dusty miller, its flowers kernels of yellow and its downy leaves more white than gray, and at the same time she was careful to hold her head high. She was battling anxiety. She neared the Smiths' cottage and spoke first, a fast hello.

Mrs. Smith smiled from a deck chair, the sun drying her washed hair. She had on shorts over her bathing suit. Mr. Smith was nowhere about. Joan came closer, and Mrs. Smith said, "I have to take the sun while I can. We're leaving soon."

"We'll miss you."

"It's nice of you to say that." Mrs. Smith's eyes seemed to fill, and her peach lipstick glistened. "All the time my husband and I have been coming here, we've never made many friends. Lyman, of course, was one. Do you mind my mentioning him?"

Joan had a faint sense of being secretly watched. "I don't mind, but—"

"I know you probably didn't like him. He wasn't everybody's cup of tea, but my husband and I were grateful to him. He helped keep our marriage together. Don't worry, I'm not going to bore you with all that nonsense."

Joan held her head oddly, like a bird shot in the neck, pain bunching up in peculiar places. She watched Mrs. Smith consult her watch and pick at the bracelet biting into her wrist.

"He used to come see us at this hour. I always washed my hair for him." Tears started in Mrs. Smith's eyes, but she swiftly controlled herself. "I wonder. Is there happiness after death? If there is, you can rest assured Lyman will get his share. The dentist, too. They were the same sort, as you might've heard. Doctor Dray used to tell me I had a beautiful voice. Teeth have a lot to do with it, he said."

Joan averted her eyes, her gaze traveling the sandy distance to the receding surf. Boulders that had been underwater smarted in the sun. Not a cloud in sight, as if the rain had never fallen. Mrs. Smith made a vague movement with her hand.

"I know you want to ask me something. I could feel it from the start."

Joan glimpsed a red yachting cap. Mr. Smith was watching from a window. She leaned forward and spoke in a low tone, a quick question that surprised Mrs. Smith, who for a moment did not react and then broke out in a smile.

"No, dear. The last I had is gone. I do business with the Farnham girl. Do you know her?"

Joan shook her head.

"I'll get some for you," Mrs. Smith said, genuinely glad to be of help.

Chief Jenkins went into a back room of the station, where Sergeant Wilbur Cox had a seventeen-year-old boy in tow. He was inking and firmly pressing the boy's fingers, one by one, on an ID card. The chief, tossing his slicker onto a chair, said, "What's he done?"

"I'll take care of it. Come on, kid, give me the other hand."

"I asked you a question, Wilbur."

"He ran a light on the boulevard." Wilbur Cox had a heavy grip on the boy, who was half the sergeant's size and shaky all over. "He mouthed off at me when I pulled him over. Then the little shit assaulted me."

The boy struggled. "That's a lie!"

"Shut up," the chief said. "Don't open your mouth again." The chief's eye ran over him, down to the nearly new Nike sneakers. "I don't know him. Where's he from, Wilbur?"

"Portsmouth."

"What's he doing around here?"

"Free country he told me."

"Let go of him. I want a better look at him."

"Look at him all you want." Wilbur Cox shoved the boy loose, and the chief stared at the thin stingy face, which was red on each side.

"Why'd you slap him around, Wilbur?"

"I didn't touch him."

"He *did!*"

"I told you to shut up."

"And he wrecked my watch," the boy said. "Punched it in with his thumb."

"Show me." The boy raised his wrist, and the chief squinted. "What kind of watch is it?"

"Timex."

"So's this." The chief ripped off his own. "Take it." The chief forced it upon him and then stepped back with a stain on his sleeve, ink from the boy's blunt fingers. "Is his license valid, Wilbur?"

"Yeah, it's valid. What the hell are you doing?"

"Get him out of here, Wilbur. Let him go."

"You're kidding!"

"I don't trust you, Wilbur. And I don't believe anything you say."

The boy bolted. Wilbur Cox, livid, let him. "I'm going to get you, Chief. So help me, I'm going to get you."

"No, Wilbur. I'm going to get you."

He knew what he should do, but he couldn't move. No muscle responded. He sat tipped back behind his desk with his eyes closed, and his mother-in-law came in and kneaded the top of his shoulders, a habit of hers he had never appreciated but never discouraged. She said, "What are you doing to yourself?"

"Alice, please. Don't ask me anything."

"You let things get to you."

He opened his eyes and saw a quarter of her face. The rain had stopped, and a wet heat had flooded the office. Sweat dribbled down his skin under his shirt. Alice Cross continued to knead. The likeness of her daughter stared at them. After all these years, the picture was still there on his desk. Periodically he considered interring it in a drawer but feared his mother-in-law would think he no longer cherished the memory of her only child.

She said, "Too much death in this town. Too much all at once. It's not fair to you."

Sometimes the picture embarrassed him. Strangers approaching his desk thought it was of his daughter. Perhaps in time they would mistake Alice Cross for his wife. His muscles tightened instead of loosening, and she pulled her hands away.

"You take all the heat for Ed Robertshaw. It makes you look foolish, Paul. People know you do his bidding. He gets the respect, and you get the ridicule."

The chief remembered the joke that went around that his wife had died in the arms of another man. It was at a dance in the grange hall, streamers up for Ed Robertshaw's re-election to the board of selectmen, and the chief—just a patrolman at the time—whispered to his wife to be a sport when Ed Robertshaw approached her for a dance. He was ladling out punch when the band abruptly stopped playing, though not all players lowered their instruments at the same time, and residual sounds of trumpet and trombone wafted into the lights. Ed Robertshaw's partner slid from his grasp. An aneurysm, a bubble in the brain that exploded—and Linda Jenkins dropped to the floor, doubtless dead before she hit it.

"Call him," Alice Cross said. "Resign. Tell him you don't need the job."

"But I do need it," the chief said simply.

Alice Cross suddenly began tugging at him, her fingers nervous. She was undoing his shirt. "Something on your sleeve," she explained. "Let me get it out or it'll stay in there forever." Lifting his arms, the chief let her do what she wanted, anything to keep their eyes from meeting. He watched her carry the shirt out of the office, and he remained at his desk, bare-chested, unlabeled. When she returned five minutes later with the shirt in hand, the offending sleeve damp but spotless, she noticed at once that the leather-framed photograph of her daughter was missing. The chief was on the phone.

"Who are you talking to?"

"Nobody," he said and replaced the receiver. His ring had not been answered. Alice Cross murmured something he didn't catch. "What?"

"The picture. I'm glad you put it away." But her eyes said otherwise. She dropped the shirt on his desk and left.

He put the shirt on but left it loose and unbuttoned. He tidied up his desktop, throwing a number of things away. Then he reached into the wastebasket to retrieve some of the items, pencils that only needed to be resharpened, a gum eraser that still had rubs left in it, a paperweight that bore his initials. Then with a certain inevitability, he picked up the phone. He punched out the same number, but this time the ring was answered.

"I don't mean to be a pest," he said, "but I was wondering if I might see you again. I know a great place for fried clams."

"I don't feel well," Joan replied. "That's the truth."

"Another time?"

"Yes," she promised. "Another time."

Pamela Comeau slipped back out of sight. She had been eavesdropping. Turning, she glimpsed Laura Kimball watching her from another room and she went to her on soft feet. "That was him," she said without inflection. Both women stood as shimmering planes of light. They each were in damp bathing suits. "Why is he so interested in Joan?"

"She's a lovely woman," Laura said reasonably.

"There's more to it than that. He's a policeman."

"But he's obviously not the usual sort. That could be in our favor."

"If it's me he's trying to get to, I'm not afraid. I can face him."

"I know you can." Laura's salty arm went around her. "Let's go back on the beach. We'll make Joan come with us."

"She doesn't feel well."

Laura did not hear her. She said, "The three of us. We'll plunge into every wave that comes along."

Twenty

Figures lying flat braided the beach. The afternoon sun was fierce, grinding into flesh. Through dark glasses, Joan watched her two friends climb the waves. She had neither the spirit nor the strength to join them. Sitting in a short-legged beach chair, she reached down and fingered a grave in the sand for a cigarette she had scarcely smoked. Behind her, children harvested noise and carried some of it to her. Before her, mothers lay stretched on their bellies, their bodies like boiled sweets. She leaned forward when a boy kicked up sand and grated her arm. Then she felt a tickling on her back, somebody finger-painting a design through the lotion and sweat, and she pivoted in the chair, thinking it was another of the children. Instead she saw Hetty Nelson's brittle face with its protruding bonework.

"How's my chum?" the old woman asked. Her dress was ancient chintz, and her sneakers were without laces. "I got something for you," she said and produced a mermaid's purse with the tendrils intact. "I found it this morning."

Joan accepted it as though she would prize it. She pulled herself out of the low chair. "Thank you, Hetty."

"I do for people I like." The old woman tottered. She was without her bonnet, her scalp burning through her meager hair. "We do for each other, don't we?" she said, casting a mysterious expression, which Joan let pass.

"Would you like to sit in my chair?"

There was a childlike shake of the head. "I can't stay in the

sun. I just wanted you to have your gift. I have to get back."
She again tottered. "My feet are funny."

Joan glanced idly in the direction of the gray house. For an
instant she thought she saw somebody on the porch, but she
wasn't sure and paid no more attention. "Would you like me
to help you?"

The old woman beamed. "Maybe when we get there, you
could rub my toes."

Joan, in a disquieting way, felt obligated.

When no one answered his knock, Chief Jenkins sprang
open the door and slipped inside. Quickly he reconnoitered
the downstairs rooms and went up the stairway. Moving on
cat's feet, he peered into each bedroom to satisfy himself that
he was alone. One bedroom drew him inside, the traces of a
sweet smell that was unmistakable. When he opened the
closet he could tell by the clothes that the room was Joan's.
He found the rolled packet of marijuana on the top shelf. He
left it there and brushed his hand through the clothing,
feeling pockets and reading labels, all with the names of nice
stores. He went to a bureau and leafed through bills bearing
her Cambridge address and forwarded here. He opened her
checkbook and read the entries. He opened drawers and re-
frained from pawing through her lingerie. Gently he jarred
the bureau out of place to see what might have fallen behind
and fished up a belt made from the skin of some reptile and a
paperback anthology of poetry, the cover slipping half away.
The inside of the cover bore an inscription in a male hand,
quite romantic and a shade erotic. Flipping pages, the chief
came across passages that had been underlined.

He wanted Pamela's room, but it was Laura's that he
edged into. It looked more like a library than a bedroom.
Neat stacks of the *Globe* and the *Times* occupied two chairs,

and books lined the top of the bureau. He scanned the titles. She seemed to like everything. From the top drawer he took out a vintage photograph clipped from a newspaper, laminated and dated. It showed Laura as a part of history, her face lunging out of a civil rights rally in Birmingham. Respectfully he returned the photograph to its place and checked her wastebasket. It contained a used panty shield, a seashell, and an empty aspirin tin.

Pamela's room seemed more feminine than the others, softer, brighter, as if she had gone to lengths to make a home away from home. He gazed at the photos of her two children, the boy younger than the girl, who was an ideal beauty. Abruptly, instinctively, he turned around and went to the neatly made bed. He didn't lift the pillow. He merely pressed his fingers hard and deep into it and felt the object beneath.

Then quickly he left.

Sergeant Wilbur Cox, fully uniformed, the visor of his cap tipped over his eyes, leaned over the high hospital bed and said, "I suppose you like it here—everybody waiting on you." His wife's face was turned on the pillow, and she acted as though she neither heard nor saw him. "Who sent the flowers?" he asked and looked at the card. "Shit, I might've known." He dumped them, and his wife's head rolled on the pillow, as though she might black out. She had been doing that lately, going under for a few seconds, little dips into a different world. She could almost do it at will. In moments of such self-absorption she could cancel out anything she wished. He said, "When are you getting out of here? I don't like the way Laurie does my shirts." He pushed at her shoulder. "Look at me when I talk."

"You're going to die, Wilbur."

"What?"

"I can feel it. I had a dream."

"You're doped up. What kind of dream?"

"The kids were crying, even Laurie. But I wasn't. I tried, but I couldn't."

"You're going soft. You're a basket case."

"You were never good to me, Wilbur. Not ever."

He shoved his knee at the side of the bed. "You think I'm going to listen to this shit you're crazy."

"Wilbur, put my flowers back," she said, too late. He was gone.

Two of the Philpott's regulars—the fellow with the bicycle clips and the one with the slack dentures—watched from behind the store's window and tried to read Chief Jenkins's lips as he spoke into the outside pay phone. They knew the call wasn't local because of the extra coins he had deposited. They watched him clamp a hand over one ear when a motorcycle pulled up and stammered in place, the driver taking his time killing the engine. They exchanged swift looks when the chief hung up.

The man wearing the bicycle clips picked his nose. "He never should've been made chief in the first place. You're supposed to be trained, and he never was."

"Got some kind of trainin' in the army. Wounded, wasn't he?"

"Wounded, hell. Busted his leg. I imagine he did that the way some guys put a bullet in their foot. Gets 'em out of the fight real fast."

They hurried out of the store into the hot sun. "Who snuffed Bud Brown, Chief? Figured that one out yet?"

"When I do, I'll let you know."

There was a nudging. "We hold our breaths, we might turn blue."

"Try it anyway," the chief said drily. He almost didn't mean to be overheard. They watched him get into the Ford. The windshield was a graveyard of insects, and two tires were now in need of air. He drove away slowly.

The man with the dentures said, "I bet I know where he's going."

"To hell," said the man with the clips.

The chief turned left and drove up Lodge Road and parked half on the sidewalk, near the roses, which were past their peak. The Corvette was in the drive. The front door was open. Cora Dray's voice came from the depths. "You can come in."

He treaded lightly over blue carpeting into a room sickeningly sweetened by an air spray. The shades were pulled. He entered another room, the same dimness, the same smell. He paused for bearings. "Where are you?" he said.

"I'm not hiding."

He went into the kitchen, where the polished floor looked like the placid surface of a lake, cool and deep. The odor of air spray was thicker. Cora stood near the open window over the sink, her tube of hair unraveled.

"I've been cleaning."

She had unbuttoned her blouse to the little breeze coming in from the window. The chief saw much cleavage. She was remote, as if particular images were flitting through her brain, occupying her. Her eyes were hooded.

"I phoned to see if Gladys Cox wanted to work for me again. But her daughter said she's in the hospital."

"She'll be there for a while."

"That's what the child said." Cora turned slightly. Her black hair draped her spine. "I have to sit down," she said, moving to a chair almost like an austere abstraction. The chief remained standing. Her voice rose up and seemed to curve around him. "When are you going to tell me who really killed my husband? It wasn't Bud."

"I know."

"Was it a woman?"

"I think so," the chief said.

"A friend of yours?"

"It could be a friend of a friend." The chief stepped nearer to the window, but the breeze had vanished. He stood with a deceptive air of being uncaring and unalert. "Do you need to know the name?"

Cora Dray shook her head. "It doesn't matter. Does that surprise you?"

"No," he said and found that now he too needed to sit down, choosing the chair farthest from hers, the length of the table separating them. His throat was dry, affecting his voice. "We have to talk about Bud."

"Why? He's better off." She lifted a hand to prevent an interruption. Her eyes were chinks, as if niched in stone. "He was never right from birth. You know that. I should kiss the hand of whoever put him out of his suffering."

"Was it Skelly?"

"Why should I tell you?"

"Cora. Did you put her up to it?"

Cora gazed through him. "You can lead a horse to water, but you can't make it drink."

"You're telling me you might have."

"I'm telling you Skelly wouldn't do anything she didn't want to."

"Cora. I need you to say it out loud. Just so there won't be any doubt in my mind."

"Of course she did it, you damn fool!"

As soon as Joan entered her room she knew that someone

had been in it. She sensed it. She felt it in every bone. She could almost see the chief's face looming over her possessions, inspecting her grass, thumbing the stubs in her checkbook, sliding drawers loose. With an air of desolation, she sat on the edge of the bed. Her fingers were pressed into her forehead when Laura came into the room. She dropped her hand and looked up with a near-normal expression.

"Has anybody been in your room?"

"I don't know," Laura said, stopping short. "I don't think so. Do you mean Pam?"

"No."

"Oh, my God. Who?"

"Him," Joan said and heard her friend's breath catch.

"Maybe he's been in Pam's room too."

"Where is she?"

"Still on the beach."

"I don't want her jumping to conclusions."

"Joan." There was an order and stillness to Laura's tall figure. "Can we prevent it?"

"I don't know."

"I'll be right back," Laura said with a suddenness and rushed out of the room with galloping strides. She was back within the minute, breathless, with almost a triumphant smile, except her long face was ghastly. "It's still there, under the pillow. Joan, that means he couldn't have been in her room. And you might only be imagining he was in yours."

"I doubt it."

Laura looked down at the floor, at her solidly tanned feet. Then she brought her eyes up slowly. "You might have to be good to him, better than you have been," she said and watched dismay and pain pass across Joan's features.

"I wouldn't know how, not in that way."

"For Pam . . . you could do it." The voice sounded

haunted. "We could do it."

Joan said nothing. Her mind felt black and blue.

"All of us," Laura added.

"*Not* Pam."

"Yes, even Pam."

At that instant Pamela appeared in the doorway, her face masked in sunglasses, her sleeveless robe tied tight. "Don't be afraid for me," she said in a light tone, as if at any moment she would turn vivacious, smiling, and happy.

Sergeant Wilbur Cox drove to Route One in his cruiser, Chief Jenkins sitting beside him, neither man speaking. It was past seven, the sun fading. Sergeant Cox rolled the cruiser soundlessly into the lot of the Mobil station and braked gently near the pumps. A mirage of water glazed the asphalt near the drawn double doors of the garage. "Shit," the sergeant said, "the place looks like it's locked tighter than a drum."

"There's a side door," the chief said tonelessly from a slightly uncomfortable posture. He blinked slowly and settled in his seat, the sergeant staring at him.

"We just going to sit here?"

"Might as well," the chief said with a strange lack of urgency. His face was dead of expression, like cement. The sergeant gave him an ugly look.

"You phoned her, didn't you?"

"That's right, Wilbur. I thought she should have the chance to come in on her own."

"That didn't happen," Sergeant Cox said with contempt.

"Still a good move," the chief said mostly in an undertone. "She's not the sort we want to surprise."

"So you figure on waiting her out?"

"You know a better way?"

The sergeant snorted. "You bet your ass I do. I'll go in and get her."

"Why make it rough on yourself?"

"What's the problem? All she is is a hunk of fat." The sergeant snapped open his door. "Two minutes. That's how long it'll take."

There was a hint of remorse and some agony in the chief's face as he said, "All right, Wilbur. But leave your weapon here."

"What? Are you kidding me?"

"I don't want you blowing her head off."

"What if she resists?"

"Use your stick."

Wilbur Cox smiled sardonically. "What do you want to do, Chief, give her a sporting chance?"

"Something like that."

Wilbur Cox pulled himself smartly out of the cruiser and with movements deliberate and ironic stripped himself of his pearl-handled service revolver. He tossed the weapon into the cruiser, where it bounced heavily on the seat. "It's an asshole way to do police work, but you're the boss."

With an odd sense of unreality the chief watched Wilbur Cox stride beyond the pumps and splash through the mirage of water and disappear around the corner of the garage. During a moment of stillness the chief felt far away, not even peripherally involved, the way he imagined Bud Brown had felt inside the coma. Then awkwardly he skewed the rearview mirror to make sure the person he saw in it was himself.

Wilbur Cox paused at the side door and lifted a pant-leg. Strapped to his hairy calf was a small dark pistol, five rounds to the clip. He released the pistol from its leather pouch and brought it close to his face to check. It smelled of oil and leather and of himself. He had fired it once, a couple of years ago, killing a gull. Surreptitiously he opened the narrow door and slipped sideways into the gloom. Skelly was there.

She was remote, glacial, and the sergeant crept in too far and saw her too late. She was behind him, and he whirled about as she lumbered toward him with a face smeared as if from crying. He said, "Whatever you've got in your hand, *drop it!*" It was a tire iron. Her breaths were heaves. "Stupid bitch!" he said and snapped off a shot. Then another. He felt certain he had hit her at least once, but she kept coming. "Damn you!" he said and fired again. She went up on her toes. With an enormous reach she swung the tire iron and broke his wrist. She swung again and broke his head.

The chief did not immediately react to the sound of gunfire. He wasn't sure it was gunfire, or rather he wanted to believe it wasn't. He righted the rearview and climbed out of the cruiser and waded through the mirage, which was real enough to make him feel wet. He wished it were deep enough to submerge his thoughts. When he got inside the garage he saw Skelly sitting on the floor as if something had pushed her there. Tummy fat bulged out of her unfastened coveralls. She still held the tire iron, which looked as if it had been painted red. Then he saw Wilbur Cox lying flat on his back. The blasted eyes told it all.

A state police car was parked near the pumps. The two young troopers, Hector and Mack, stood with their arms crossed in the narrowing light. Lieutenant Haas moved close to the chief and stood menacingly near, as if he wanted no air between them. He stared at the chief and said, "You mind telling me what happened?"

"She didn't realize who he was. She thought he was a burglar."

"What kind of crap you handing me?"

"Usually it's the other way around," the chief murmured. "How's it feel?"

The lieutenant started to say something and stopped himself, and he began looking at the chief in a different way. The chief, aware of shadows piling up, scrunched a shoe on the asphalt. "You in her corner?" the lieutenant asked. Receiving no response, he said, "Why not? Everybody's in someone's corner. That's the way we survive."

"I wouldn't know," the chief said. "I'm not that experienced."

"You do all right."

"You can have her for Bud Brown. What more do you want?"

"I didn't know I wanted her for anything until you told me," the lieutenant said dryly. From a distant point on Route One came the wail of an ambulance.

The chief said, "That's for her. I think she's wounded."

"You sure she's a woman? I looked in there, I couldn't tell." Lieutenant Haas gave a curt signal, and the two troopers dropped their arms and moved toward the garage. They had on their tall hats, which made them look more than ever like Texas Rangers. The chief eyed them stiffly as they passed by.

"Be gentle," he said.

Lieutenant Haas displayed a slow grin, a playful touch of respect in his eyes, the kind of respect the chief didn't want. The wail of the ambulance grew louder, and the chief turned his face away from the lieutenant's.

"Confidentially, Chief," Lieutenant Haas spoke with mild amusement and curiosity. "If you wanted to get rid of your sergeant why didn't you just fire him?"

Twenty-one

Chief Jenkins did not sleep that night. He did not even go home. He drove the cruiser down Route One to Ninety-Five. There was a thunderstorm, a small one, when he crossed into Massachusetts. He tightened his hold on the wheel and sped through the rain, the tires hissing as if the bottom of the cruiser were boiling. It had rained harder in Boston. The puddles were bigger, prismatic in the streetlight. He drove to a poor neighborhood in the Brighton section, three-decker tenement houses, not all of them shabby.

He climbed the stairs and knocked on a door several times before it creaked open. A man with wisps of prematurely white hair and a Mickey Rooney face peered out at him. "You who I think you are?" he said with much surprise and opened the door wide. His name was Nelligan, a detective with the Boston Police Department, District Fourteen. He and the chief had been in the army together, Korea. It was Nelligan who had raced for a medic when the chief had fallen from the back of the truck. "Jesus Christ, come in!"

The kitchen was oversized, the biggest room in the tenement, and full of shadows because only a small light was on. A very young woman appeared from another room and stopped short. She was barefooted and wearing Nelligan's bathrobe. "She's a neighbor," Nelligan whispered, a shade abashed. His wife had died several years ago, and the chief had gone to the funeral. "You want some coffee, Paul? The kid will make some." The chief shook his head, and Nelligan raised his eyes. "Leave us alone, honey, and shut the door."

They sat at a chrome-legged table, the top unwiped where sandwiches had been made. The chief was careful where he placed his elbows. "I'm sorry to bother you at this hour."

"I'm glad to see you anytime, Paul."

"I tried to reach you during the day at the station, but you weren't in."

"I was here. What do you want, Paul?"

"I need you to do something for me. Some checking." The chief removed a slip of paper from his shirt pocket. "Here's the name."

Nelligan read the name. He didn't recognize it. The chief had not expected he would. "Lives here in the city?" Nelligan asked.

"Yes."

"She mean something to you, Paul?"

"Friend of a friend."

"Do you want to confide?"

"No." The chief used a forearm to rub perspiration from his face. "You might not come up with anything."

"But you want me to try."

"I do."

"Where do you want me to call you, Paul?"

"I'll call you."

Nelligan walked the chief to the door and partway down the stairs. "The kid, Paul, you'd like her if you knew her."

The chief said, "I like her without knowing her."

Pamela, who'd had a restless night, stood at the porch rail. She was unsure whether she wanted to go onto the beach. Only eight o'clock, and already the sun seemed capable of annihilation. She gave sidelong looks at Laura watering the fuchsia and at Joan quietly sipping coffee. "Something's wrong," she said in a sudden torment of anxiety. "You both are too quiet."

Laura feigned surprise, and Joan said, "Everybody's quiet this early. The whole world is."

"You two were talking last night. Late. I heard you."

"That was my fault," Laura said quickly. "I woke up from a bad dream and went in to tell Joan about it."

"Tell *me* about it."

Laura hesitated. "Silly dream really. My husband showed up bold as brass and claimed he was no longer homosexual. He said he had his own church again and was going straight, and did I want him back. The macabre part was that his friend was with him, holding his hand."

Pamela looked sharply away and said into the air, "Don't leave me out of things."

"No one is." Joan had spoken sharply, as if she'd felt she had to, and Pamela pulled back.

"You're the only ones I trust."

Joan placed her coffee cup on the rail and swiftly went to her. She was about to curve an arm around her, but Pamela stepped back, withdrawing into a defensive rigidity. Joan spoke quietly. "Are you going to manage?"

"Yes."

"You're going to hold up."

"Yes. Don't fuss."

Joan set her shoulders. She did not look her best, her thick hair thoughtlessly brushed, her eyes swollen. Her voice dipped. "I think you should get rid of what's under the pillow. It's time."

"It's never time," Pamela murmured, looking at nobody. Laura drew near.

"I'll get rid of it for you if you like. I'll get in the Volks. I'll drive off somewhere and find a bridge."

"It's not under the pillow," Pamela said. "I don't know where it is now. I've hidden it." She slipped away from the rail, the sleeveless robe wrapped around her, and announced, "I'm going down to the beach."

Carrying a folded deck chair, she angled through an almost unbearable brightness. The sand caved in under her clogs. Some children floated in and out of her line of vision, all smiling at her, as if she were one of them and would join them in play. Their father was nearby with a beach ball, which tumbled from his hands and rolled against her foot. She kicked it back to him. When he smiled his thanks through fleshy lips, her stomach turned, as if he were inflicting some silent indignity upon her.

She had a headache. Perhaps it started that instant. She brought a hand to her forehead and pushed at the skin, which was tightening. The sun was doing it. She carried the chair close to the surf for the subtle change of texture in the air. The chair had a tendency to stick, and she struggled to erect it, then collapsed in it, keeping her robe tight about her and stretching her feet. The children dashed by into the breaking surf, and their father, toting the beach ball, followed. He splashed beyond them and took a great lick of water between the legs as a wave broke. Pamela glanced up without surprise when a shadow fell near.

"I knew you wouldn't let it rest," she said.

"You forgot these." Joan clutched sunglasses.

"Thank you."

"Can't we talk?"

Pamela put on the glasses and directed her gaze back to the surf, more bathers in it now. Joan had dropped to a knee and was speaking quietly, but she wasn't listening. It wasn't the time, maybe not even the place. "Look at that man," she said, softly interrupting.

Joan's head pivoted. "Which one?"

"With the beach ball. Tell me that isn't Roger smiling out of that face."

"No," Joan said at once. "It doesn't even look like him."

"The one with the children. See!"

"No," Joan said roughly. "Roger's gone."

Unshaved, the chief drank coffee at his desk. The door was closed. He did not want to be disturbed, but Alice Cross came in anyway. She was tense. He had no fear that she would knead his neck, for she kept her distance.

"Paul."

"Yes, Alice, I'm listening."

"Ed Robertshaw will be at his shack most of the morning. He wants to see you."

"I'm not seeing anybody."

"Paul, he wants you to resign." Her voice was well-controlled, but her face wasn't. "He said it's for your own good."

"Call him back, Alice. Tell him I'm not resigning, and he'd better think twice about firing me."

Alice Cross staggered to a chair near the desk. The chief thought she was going to sink into the chair, but she merely gripped the back. "I phoned the hospital," she said, eyes censoring him. "They say she was definitely wounded in three places, but they can't find the bullets. All that fat."

"That's almost funny, isn't it?" he said, his words traducing his feelings. He considered getting up, but that seemed to call for a strength beyond the possibilities of his body. "Cora will get her the best lawyer money can buy."

"How do you know that?"

"I'm guessing."

"What are you guessing for Gladys Cox? What does she get?"

"She has benefits coming, Alice. You'll do the paperwork. Big dollars. We'll make sure of that, won't we?"

Alice's knuckles whitened over her grip on the back of the chair. Her eyes locked into his, as if to stare him out. "Tell me what happened at the gas station," she said and watched him sigh.

"Bess Cook typed out my report. I'm sure you read it this morning." He opened a drawer. "I have a copy here if you haven't."

"Paul." She spoke with a kind of bloodlessness. Her careful hair, for once, was not all in place. Dispersing strands clung to both cheeks. "I don't think you're telling the whole story."

"What makes you think that, Alice?"

"Maybe I know you as my daughter never did."

The chief spoke into his coffee cup. "Wilbur wanted to hang himself and took the rope right out of my hand."

Later, alone, frozen in a stiff posture of stagnation, he stared at the telephone as if he might suddenly snatch it up, but three or four minutes passed before he reached for it. And his movement was slow and deliberate. He called the gray house. Laura answered and told him Joan was unavailable.

"Is she feeling better?"

"Yes, she is. She's gone food shopping." Laura's tone was genial, obliging, calm. "I'm not sure when she'll be back. Shall I have her call you?"

"I don't know where I'll be," the chief said.

Joan got out of her little Volkswagen and moved with purpose toward Chief Jenkins's house. Behind her, spectral light chipped through the pines. The sky was acid-green and the air muggy, cluttered with mosquitoes. The chief glimpsed her from a window, for him a heart-swelling moment. She climbed the stout steps to his porch, and he opened the door. There was an eerie moment of silence when their eyes connected, as if the silence were feeding on itself. She was in shorts, and he was conscious of her large dark legs, also of the fatigue in her face, the same kind marking his. Somberly she said, "Are you trying to drive me crazy?"

He played dumb.

"You were in our house," she said as mosquitoes tore at her legs.

"Come in, please."

She entered his kitchen. He wanted her to sit, but she shook her head. "You were in my room." He didn't admit it, but he didn't deny it either. She said, "Do you know what it's like having a stranger invade your property?"

He started to speak but checked himself and stood stiff-necked, his lack of sleep beginning to tell. Then abruptly he stepped away and opened a cupboard. "There's wine here. The bottle I told you about."

Some was missing. It was on his breath. His back to her, he poured out two glasses, and she took a chair at the table, not because she wanted to but because her legs were giving. He keyed open a can of sardines and began making small moist sandwiches.

"I can't believe you're doing that," she said.

"I'm hungry," he said, "and I was hoping you'd join me." He turned around, his eyes full upon her. "I was also hoping you'd relax."

She stared, trying to find something about him she could like and choosing his mouth, sensitive, soft-looking, fine enough for a woman and yet fitting for a man.

He dumped potato chips into a bowl. Presently he carried

a tray to the table and sat near her, half-smiling. "Maybe we can forget everything for a while and enjoy each other's company."

"What am I supposed to say to that?" There was a plate before her, a sliver of pickle on the sandwich. The wine was in a water glass. "I don't want your food."

"It's there if you do," he said and began to eat, small bites, his eyes slipping over her. "Why," he mused with almost a laugh, "do we go to such extremes for others? Is it actually for ourselves?"

"I don't understand the question."

"Yes, you do," he said gently. From beyond the pines came the sound of a passing car and of a bottle breaking on the road. "Kids," he said. "The worst thing about them is the mess they make. Second is the noise."

"Please don't tell me what I do or don't understand," she said, and her stillness seemed to disconcert him. She was coolheaded, but she felt her face become drawn.

"Try the wine," he coaxed, and she did, for her throat was dry. He had provided napkins, and she used one. He said, "I think it important I talk to Mrs. Comeau, don't you agree?"

"No," she said and watched him finish his sandwich. "I don't agree at all."

"It might help me."

"I don't see how." There was a calculated pause. "I've told you she's not strong. Laura and I would be willing to pay you money just to leave her alone."

"I'm not interested in money. You couldn't guess how little I spend."

She turned her head to free herself of his eyes. Her shirt showed a sweat patch under each arm, and her hair, gripped in a rubber band behind her head, had come loose at the sides. He watched her take another taste of wine and again use a napkin. The first one had fallen through her legs.

"Don't be afraid of me," he said. "Please don't be afraid. I think what I'm doing is asking for your help."

Instead of responding, she rose stiff and cramped and tried hard to be matter of fact. "May I use your bathroom?" she asked, and he at once indicated the direction. She moved as if on a slow wheel, and he twisted in his chair.

"The switch is on the outside."

She locked herself in and went to the sink, dashing her hands under water and dousing her face. Without drying herself, she unknotted the rubber band and let her hair fall loose. Then she picked at the buttons on her shirt and the zipper on the side of her shorts. A moment or so later, as she tried to assume an easeful stance, the mirror duly recorded her nakedness. Soundlessly she lifted the lock on the door, but when she reached for the knob she found her courage used up. Now she wanted to cry.

A good five minutes passed before she emerged from the bathroom, her hair back in the grip of the band, her hands wedged in the side pockets of her shorts. The chief was no longer in the kitchen. He had committed himself to the deepest chair in his den. She looked in at him and said, "Sorry for taking so long."

"Now can we talk?"

"Not this moment," she said and was out of the house before he could protest.

Twenty-two

Once again Chief Jenkins drove to Boston, though he could have just as easily picked up the telephone for the information. He needed the delay of the drive, and the drive itself, again using the cruiser, not trusting the Ford that far beyond the boundaries of Boar's Bluff, as if the Ford were an unreliable extension of himself and the cruiser a more aggressive one.

The district station in Brighton, nearing abandonment under a reorganization, was forbidding from the outside and decrepit and dank inside. Officers, uniformed and otherwise, drifted sluggishly by him, bellies on most of them, every other face geriatric. He knew his way, glad he didn't have to ask. He didn't think they'd tell him. Nelligan sat behind a grimy desk delicately peeling apart a wrapper on a sandwich, bologna with lettuce leaking out. He had on an old polo shirt and looked as if he belonged in a tavern, a foot on the rail. Showing no surprise when the chief pulled up a chair, he gave a little shove at the sandwich and said, "Have half. The kid made it."

It took the chief a second to remember who "the kid" was and another second to conjure up the small wan face. He wondered whether she had a name.

"She wants me to marry her—can you beat that? For my sake, she says. She thinks I'm getting weird living alone."

"Why don't you marry her?"

"Hell, Paul. The age difference. She says it doesn't have to

213

be forever. For me, that is forever."

"Then do it."

"I might." He pushed at the other half of the sandwich. "Eat this too. I don't really want it."

The chief shook his head. "Thanks, anyway."

Nelligan leaned forward on his elbows to look at the chief's weaponless waist. "Never did like guns, did you? Not even in the army."

"You never did either."

"For me now, it's different. As far as I'm concerned, the biggest weapon in the world is a sawed-off double-barrel shotgun. The only time I saw one used I thought the building was coming down. I still got the noise in my ears, but I never put in for disability. I learned to live with it."

The chief was quiet. He wiped his mouth, and Nelligan gave him an unexpected smile.

"The time you fell off the truck and broke your leg. I always wondered. Did you do that on purpose?"

"That's too far back for me to remember," the chief said and gazed beyond Nelligan. "That's when a book of matches carried the strip for striking on the front, not the back."

Nelligan said, "I guess you want to talk about this Comeau woman."

"I do."

"Lives in Brookline. Great neighborhood. Perry Street. I want to make sure it's the right person."

"I'm sure it is."

"It's not a pretty story."

"I didn't think it would be," the chief said.

"I don't know where he is and have no idea when he'll be back," Alice Cross said sharply, trying to hide her nervousness. "What's so important, Leo?"

Officer Leo Morin tugged at his cap, squaring it in a manner reminiscent of Wilbur Cox, except the young officer's cap was oversized and unflattering, his ears protruding. "I'm thinking of quitting," he said, and Alice instantly turned more attentive. "Actually," he said, "I've pretty much made up my mind."

"Do you want to talk about it?"

"I don't know what there is to talk about. I'm just not cut out to be a cop."

"Is that all there is to it?"

Leo Morin's face grew pink. He said, "My mother doesn't think I should work for him anymore."

"The chief?"

"I don't think I should either."

Alice rose from her chair. "This is a terrible time, Leo, for all of us. For the chief especially. Think about him for a moment, Leo. He always treated you decently. Remember the time you cut up in the cruiser on the back roads? If anybody else had been chief, you'd have been fired on the spot. Does your mother know about that? Does she know about the time you discharged your weapon behind the Fotomat just to impress a girl?"

Officer Morin looked down at the floor and scuffed a shoe. At the same time he hitched up his trousers. Alice sighed as though from deep aches.

"Do you have to quit this minute? This day? Can't you stay on for a little longer?"

He glanced up, sheepish and conciliatory. "I guess I can do that."

"Good," Alice said. "You might even outlast him."

For the first time since her husband's death Cora Dray appeared on the beach and stood where the ocean washed

215

against boulders and sucked into crevices. The sound was unsettling, like hearing a man thrash, gurgle, and die. The sun gnawed at her. She wore the heat hard, and her high and heavy hairdo looked set to slip off her head. Her senses sharpened when a shadow fell near her. "This is where it happened?" she asked without determining whom she was addressing. A slender arm went up, and a finger pointed.

"Over there."

Cora turned slowly. "Do I know you?"

"The gray house," Pamela said, a tilted figure, as if misdrawn. Cora nodded.

"Canucks were there last year. You're a better breed, fancy. You and your friends shine out from the crowd, especially you. I suppose my husband noticed you. No way he wouldn't have." She smiled tightly and said with complete certainty, "But you didn't give him a tumble. Too classy for him, I can tell. That must've burned him."

Pamela's mouth opened but produced no sound. Salt air pressed against her face, and the sun maintained a fire on her back. Her bathing suit was cut high on the hip, Cora's eyes bit in.

"You have a lovely shape. I never had one like that, not even when I was eighteen years old." The winking brightness of the sea hurt her eyes, and she shaded them. "You don't have to feel sorry for me. I loved my husband, but he was a prick."

"I'll talk about him if you want," Pamela said in a voice that came from the depths, an unsure decision made, but her voice did not penetrate the din of Cora's thoughts.

"He was an idiot. I don't mean like my brother. My poor brother was a baby." She repulsed the threat of tears. "Did you know Bud? No, I guess you wouldn't have, but he probably knew you."

Pamela tried again, moving closer. "Your husband," she started to say and detected only the smallest air of interest and then none. Her tower of hair listing, Cora seemed strangely at peace, as if she knew enough and wanted no more to deal with. Water swarmed up and thickened around their ankles, cool and comforting.

"I'm keeping my brother's car but selling my husband's. Do you want to buy it? A Cadillac." Their eyes met, a message in Cora's. "The price will be right."

Pamela, her feet sucked into the drenched sand, reached out. The hand did not touch the other woman. It stayed in the air. "No," she said, "but thank you so much."

The sun irradiated the sand. Half blinded by the glare, Chief Jenkins fretfully searched for a dusty-pink bathing suit, but Joan was wearing a white one, which did not entirely cover the ghost of the old one. She was on a towel, on her side, one knee thrust out. The chief knelt beside her. When she looked up, he carefully removed her sunglasses. "You don't look well," he said with concern. "You don't look yourself."

"Maybe it's the sun, or something I ate. Maybe it's you." She took time in forming her words. "I'm exceptionally tired. It happens."

"Yes. When you haven't slept. I haven't either."

"It's not a question of sleep." She wanted her glasses back, but the chief kept them close to his chest and continued to peer down at her. She shielded her eyes with her hand, but the sun pricked through her fingers. "I suppose I was expecting you, but not at this moment."

"I didn't expect you to leave so abruptly last evening," he said lightly and returned the sunglasses. "I had to finish the wine myself."

"You could have called Winnie Wallace. She's your friend, isn't she?"

"Yes, my very good friend."

"Do you love her?" Joan asked, as if she really wanted to know. She was sitting up now, with her arms around her knees, rocking a little.

"I care for her," the chief said. "I don't love her."

"Do you love anybody?"

"I could love you. Astounding I should say that, but it could be true."

"You're a lonely man."

"Not as much as people seem to think."

"Is this something I should be hearing?" It was a serious question from a third voice, startling the chief, who wavered in his crouch. A short distance away Laura lay flat, encased in the glare, and he immediately felt obtuse for not having noticed her. She picked herself up and caught hold of the hot sand with her toes. She stood tall, with balance and clarity, longer in the leg than he had remembered, her handsome teeth a shade too big for her mouth.

"You don't have to leave," he said.

She said, "The ocean beckons."

Together he and Joan watched her hoof it to the surf, where she leaned forward and sloshed water over her arms and shoulders in a manner almost ritualistic. Then, long-legged, she sliced deeper into the surf and confronted a wave that jolted her up, threw her high, and let down gently. The chief said, "I should've brought my bathing suit."

"Next time," Joan said, and the chief gave her a side look as if next time were too tenuous a thought. She dropped back on an elbow, her head drooping and her hair crumpling over the towel. "Sometime," she said, "put your ear to the sand. It will whisper to you."

"What will it say?"

"Whatever you want."

"Will it tell me about the man who hurt Mrs. Comeau?"

Joan's expression did not change, but her body did, as if every muscle had tightened. "What man?"

"Roger."

A jet appeared on the horizon. It looked like lead, a super bullet, and a moment later the sky turned thundery. Joan lifted herself off her elbow and tightened loose straps. Boys breezed by, watching. She readjusted her sunglasses as a gull shivered overhead and then flew off.

The chief said, "I'm not sure of his last name. He seems to have had more than one."

"How did you find out about him?"

"I have a contact in the Boston Police Department."

"What do you know?"

The chief timed his words. "He's a missing person."

Laura waded out of the surf and came forward in a smooth flow, a scrap of seaweed clinging to an ankle. She dried one arm and then the other in a blue towel and then, bending double and revealing breasts with some heft to them, did her legs.

Joan said, "We were talking about Roger."

"How odd," Laura said calmly. "I thought you might be."

Joan and the chief strolled along the surf where the sand was moist and mushy and charted the beach with wet footprints. The chief carried his desert boots in his hands, black stockings hotly stuffed inside. Joan said, "Roger was somebody she met after her divorce."

"I was told he looked as if he were impersonating a Harvard student, nineteen-fifties. Handsome fellow, but probably older than he looked. How did she meet him?"

"How isn't important. When is. When she was most vulnerable." Joan took a few fast steps ahead of him and then
gazed off while waiting for him to catch up. The ocean reared
up its silver swell, whitecaps jittering. "He came across as
self-effacing, gentle, but he was hardly that. After he charmed
her, made her feel like a woman again, he began abusing her.
There was damage to her kidneys. She was in Mass General
for a time."

"The investigating officer wanted to prosecute, but she
was uncooperative."

"Is that so hard to understand?" Joan looked at him fleet-
ingly. "She was ashamed. Ashamed she'd ever known him."

"He also did something to her daughter. He raped her.
Why didn't she follow through and then prosecute? She was
going to. She was ready to sign the complaint."

"For the sake of the child. She wanted to shield her from
any more horror, and her ex-husband flew in from Seattle
and agreed with her. He took the girl back with him, and the
boy. She's alone now. Laura and I are all she has." Joan
shoved her hair back with both hands and gave him a full
look. "And we don't intend to desert her."

"I didn't think so," the chief said. Their steps were slow,
his crooked, the bum knee acting up. He said, "I know what's
under her pillow."

"For protection," Joan said quickly. "After what she's
been through, can you blame her? She's never used it, probably doesn't even know how."

"I don't know if I can believe that," he said, looking off.
Distant waves carried a sturdy sailboat. Nearer ones accom-
modated gulls. "I left the weapon where it was because I
didn't have the authority to take it. Sometimes I really do play
by the rules."

"I don't know what your rules are."

"I don't always either."

"Then I wonder if the world is wired for a policeman like you."

His knee buckled, and he stopped to rub it. The cap felt like a ball of iron. "Damn it," he said softly. "Damn it. Damn it."

"What's the injury?" she asked.

"A very old one." He stood erect, his desert boots hanging heavily from one hand, the heels run down. His face altered slightly, along with his voice. "Where is Roger now?"

"The one to ask is Pamela, but I can tell you she doesn't know."

"We have to talk," he said, measuring out the words, and she looked at him precisely and accurately. "All of us, I mean."

"I know what you mean," she said, and they reversed direction and began trudging the distance to the gray house.

Pamela Comeau bought a pack of no-name generic cigarettes in Philpott's and then joined Laura Kimball at the deli counter, where they picked out meats and cheeses before moving along to the bakery display. Later, on Route One, they stopped for gasoline at Skelly's Mobil, but the place was closed, padlocks on the doors, chains around the pumps; so they drove to the Texaco station down the line. Afterward they went to the state liquor store.

Joan Weiss, in the meantime, climbed the stairs to her bedroom while the chief waited downstairs in a chair. She wriggled out of her bathing suit, laid out a dress and underwear on the bed, and then slipped into the bathroom to shower. She took her time.

The chief, fatigued from not enough sleep and too much sun, dozed off a couple of times in the deep chair, which was situated in a dim corner of the room. The room was on a far side of the house, isolated from others, and well away from the porch. Vaguely he heard Joan come out of the bathroom and expected her to reappear shortly, but she didn't. Finally he made his way through one room and then two others to the foot of the stairs and called up to her. She said she'd be down soon. He said, "Where are the others? You said they'd be right back."

"They will be."

He returned to his chair, pulling it out of the corner and pushing it near a window, where an ocean breeze billowed the curtain. He sank heavily into the chair and closed his eyes. When he opened them, the light in the room had declined considerably. The slam of a car door told him that Laura and Pamela had returned, and later he heard them enter a distant part of the house. Joan's footsteps sounded on the stairs and died away after reaching bottom. He figured they had all gathered in the kitchen, and he waited some more. Eventually Joan entered the room alone.

"It's getting dark in here," she said, and click went a switch. Light from a small lamp spread into a small portion of the room. She was frocked in a cool color with a modest décolletage and stood shapely and large-limbed. "We hope you're hungry."

"You don't have to feed me," he said.

"It's no trouble," she said in a tone that prevented argument.

"I wonder if—"

"Of course," she said, anticipating, and directed him to the downstairs john. Fresh towels were laid out by the sink, as if especially for him, along with an untouched bar of Zest soap. The mirror gave him an oddly swollen look. When he returned to the room, the women were setting up a buffet table. His eyes seemed to sort and measure them as they laid out dishes of cold cuts, slabs of cheese, various dark breads, condiments, wine. Slim and imperiously pure in a lacy shirt, Pamela gave out a faint smile that did not seem to include him. Lamplight pierced her linen skirt, and he admired her legs. Laura had on a strapless top, her shoulders shining.

"Sit down," Joan said. "I'll fix you a plate."

It was more an order than an offer, and he obeyed with a perfunctory air, as if he were now playing everything by ear.

"I hope this is enough," she said, giving him a generous serving. He sat straight and balanced the plate on his knees. She shifted an end table to accommodate his glass of wine. Pamela and Laura shared a sofa, only token amounts on their plates. The only stiffness was in their smiles. Laura asked what he did here in the winter, and he told her he checked summer homes for breaks and read *Time* magazine. She brought up the propinquity of Pease Air Force Base, spoke negatively of Ronald Reagan and fatalistically of nuclear war, and mentioned the religious right. "The world blows in the name of Jesus," she said more to the others than to him.

The chief said, "You sound angry."

She said, "No. Frightened."

He let his gaze wander to Pamela, who did not avoid his eyes but let them work slowly over her face. It was as if he were looking for some detail he might have missed. Her short neat blond hair was impeccably kept, her expression formal. She seemed quietly wound up, ready to tick fast or give out. From an armchair Joan said to him, "How are you doing?"

"Fine." He had an appetite and ate to repletion.

A stillness prevailed. He was conscious of passing time, each layer of seconds, and finally, in an undertone to Joan, he said, "I think it's time."

She was suddenly on her feet. "Let us clean up first," she said and for one small moment rested a hand on his lean and sinewy arm. Laura took away his plate. With swift efficiency, Pamela cleared the table. Joan leaned close, her breasts asserting themselves through the thin material of her frock, and refilled his wine glass. "To finish off the bottle," she said.

Then he was alone again.

Between intervals of quiet he heard water running in the kitchen and things being put away. Faintly, by pricking his ears, he heard some subdued sort of argument or debate but nothing he could make sense of. It began to rain, a thin shower, and he listened to that. When he lifted his eyes, Laura was making a place for herself on the sofa.

"I understand you were in Pamela's room," she said in a neutral tone. She was sitting casually, a wedge of white silk visible between her long thighs. "Wasn't that illegal?"

"Very much so," he conceded.

"And you were probably in mine as well."

"I have to plead guilty."

"Isn't that what you want Pamela to do?"

He did not answer directly. Instead, after letting a silence accumulate, he said, "It's got to stop."

"Are we talking business?" she asked after a similar delay.

The chief nodded heavily. His head felt heavy. "I suppose we are," he said almost too quietly for her to hear.

"And you want Pamela present."

"It's essential."

"She'll be here shortly. She's taking something for a small headache." There was a tiny noise from the kitchen, nothing recognizable. "But you're going to fall asleep."

"No, I'm not."

"Yes, you are," she said.

And he did.

★ ★ ★ ★ ★

Officer Leo Morin cruised the boulevard through the gloom of rain. He immediately slowed down when he made out the chief's car parked near the gray house. His curiosity piqued, he inched by the house while trying to see through the dimly lit windows. A number of thoughts flitted through his head. One was that the chief was investigating a break, another that the chief's car had simply broken down, which had happened on Route One last spring.

Much further up the boulevard, a fog swirling in off the ocean, he pulled into the lot of the Coral Motel and parked facing out so that he could keep an eye on the road. Sinking a little in his seat, he unwrapped a sandwich his mother had made him. Traffic at the motel was momentarily brisk. Cars arrived ghoulishly through the gloom, headlights barely visible. Halfway through the sandwich he had a wild thought. Perhaps another homicide had been committed and the chief was handling it all on his own.

At considerable risk he gunned the cruiser back onto the boulevard and activated the dome light, though he extinguished it before he reached the gray house. The chief's car was still there, but the house was darker, a single faint light showing. Now Officer Morin had another thought. Maybe the chief had himself a woman. The cruiser idled in place, the fog rolling over it. After due consideration, he decided that whatever was happening in the house was none of his business, and he sped away.

Much earlier in the evening Winnie Wallace met with a prosperous-looking couple from New York and showed them property on Robandy Road, which was in the Strawberry Drive area. "Nicest neighborhood in town," she told them. The house was an oversized garrison with a three-stall garage and space for a boat. Flagstones found their way to the door-step, and flower boxes underscored windows. The couple liked what they saw, and the husband whispered, "You're in for an easy sale. We can't take the city anymore, too dangerous."

"We have a police chief who looks after everybody," Winnie said coolly and professionally. She took the couple to dinner at the Exeter Inn, and during dessert the man made an offer she knew the seller would not refuse. "I think you have yourself a house," she said. "Welcome to our town."

The wife said, "You look very tired, dear. You really didn't have to take us to dinner."

"My pleasure," Winnie said, still the professional.

The rain had petered out and the fog was dissipating by the time she drove back alone to Boar's Bluff. A good portion of the moon illuminated the boulevard. The gray house was dark, all shades pulled. She also saw the chief's car.

He woke gradually, his head stuffy, with no idea how long he had slept, for he had no watch to tell the time. The room was dark. Forcing himself out of the chair, he stood quiet and still to get his bearings. He remembered that no lamp was within reach and with groping steps sought the one that had been on. A voice said, "Please don't put on the light."

The voice, Laura's, came from the depths of the room. Her face, which he barely made out, loomed in the dim.

"We're ready to do business, Chief. Whatever it takes."

He stepped to a window and raised the shade. Moonlight crashed in. Laura stood in a thin nightgown, her breasts exclamatory. Pamela, wearing the sleeveless robe, waited to be seen.

"What's going on?" he asked.

Laura said, "We'll do whatever's necessary to make you leave us alone."

"Forever!" Pamela added.

The chief's eyes moved here, there. "Where's Joan?"

"Won't I do?" Laura's smile was constant, unvarying. "I'll be a bitch, a tease, whatever suits you. Fair enough? Pam, what will you be for him?"

"This isn't the way," he said. "It won't solve anything."

"It will if you let it."

"I can't do that. Everything about it is wrong."

Pamela sighed abruptly. "Then tell us what's right."

He turned his back on them and peered out the window. The moon was full, an excuse for madness. "I don't know," he said and went silent. When he turned from the window, they were gone.

Later he climbed the stairs.

The door to Laura's room was closed tight, perhaps locked. Pamela's door was ajar. Her room was dark, but he could see her standing in it like a pale figure in a photograph, or rather like a shape in a negative held up to the light. He whispered, "Anything you want to tell me, I'll listen to. I'll listen to it all."

There was no response, no movement.

He tried again. "I'm not Roger. I'm not anything like him."

Then he crept to Joan's room.

"You could have at least knocked," she said, a faint light touching her. She lay on the bed in an old T-shirt and mesh briefs that did not reach her tan line. Her wraith of hair covered her pillow into which her head was sunk deep. For awhile they stared mutely at each other.

"What did you do, draw lots on me?" he asked.

"I was against it, but I went along."

He slid the chair close to the bed. It was a rocker with a braided cushion tied to the seat. It creaked when he sat in it.

She said, "We thought we could appeal to your darker side. It obviously hasn't worked."

"What did you put in my wine?"

"One of Pam's sedatives," she answered without guilt. "We needed more time to talk, to discuss."

He took a long unobscured view of her. "Maybe it would have worked if it had been you."

"It was a bad plan," she said softly. "We aren't even sure how much you know."

"I know everything."

"Perhaps you only think you do."

"You and I," he said with unexpected difficulty, "have talked about Roger as if Mrs. Comeau had been the only one involved with him. But you were too, weren't you?"

Seconds of silence passed. "What makes you so sure?" she asked with no apparent emotion.

"Behind your bureau is a paperback with an inscription. It's to you, and it's from him. Lots of love, it said, among other things. It was funny the way I found myself growing jealous." He swallowed with care. "I would guess Mrs. Kimball was not a stranger to him either."

Joan hiked herself up some, doubling the pillow behind her. She was heavy around the eyes. "I should have thrown the book away. I meant to, but there were poems I liked in it, certain passages."

"You underscored them," he said. "I didn't like them, one line in particular. Probably why I remember it. 'Death, the engraver, puts forward his bone foot.' "

"Ugly, really, isn't it, but so graphic. Robert Lowell." She appeared to smile. "You're right, of course, about Roger. At different times we each thought we loved him. It was easy to do."

"But later you hated him."

"That was even easier."

"I have to believe he's dead."

"Shouldn't you have a tape recorder?"

"Who killed him?"

"We all did," she said with deadening casualness.

Twenty-three

He rubbed his watchless wrist and asked her what time it was. At first he did not believe her when she told him. He thought it was much later and wondered if somehow they had widened the night beyond its true scope. Rocking ever so lightly in the chair, he asked, "Was it the same weapon that was used on the dentist and Lyman Arnold?"

"Yes," she said almost insouciantly, "the same weapon."

"Are there others I don't know about?"

"One other," she said, and her voice, neither hard nor soft but neutral, chilled him. "In Vermont. A boating instructor. Last summer we had a chalet on a lake. Natural springs. As far as I know his body never came up."

The chief's head swayed against the back of the rocker, as if too much of a piercing nature were devolving on him. He licked the corner of his mouth, hard.

She said, distantly, "You'd have an awful time trying to prove anything against all three of us. Would you compromise?" She paused, on purpose, looking at him now. "Settle for one of us. A full confession."

"One of you?" he said, full of mysterious muscle ache, and then he asked the obvious question.

"It can't be Pam," she said. "If you locked her up, she'd go catatonic. She's the most determined of us, but she's also the most delicate. And it can't be Laura. She's been through as much as Pam, and I don't know how strong she is either."

230

"I see. You want to be a martyr for every wronged woman in the world."

"You don't have to worry," she said evenly. "No statues will be built."

Twisting in the rocker, the chief brought his face forward and vaguely gestured in the dimness to another part of the room. "I know what you have on the closet shelf. I never pictured you as a pot smoker."

"I can't imagine that shocking you."

"It doesn't. I figure it's medicinal." He watched her go absolutely still, her face carefully arranged to reveal nothing. He spoke almost lightly. "I mentioned my contact with the Boston police. A very old buddy of mine, Nelligan. He lost his wife a few years ago. I went to the funeral. He had gone into hock trying to save her. He'd gotten the best doctor, a name everybody knows, but the doctor could only tell him how much time she had left."

Joan's voice went icy. "Make your point."

"I'm sorry," the chief said. "But I've been through your checkbook. That doctor's name kept popping up. Terribly big amounts."

"Damn you," she said with grudging respect and a tinge of relief. "You even know my ace in the hole."

He nodded. "You always knew it was there to play if the three of you were found out."

She was silent.

He said, "Do the others know you're dying?"

"No."

"What kind of cancer?" he asked.

"What difference?"

"Like your mother's?"

"Yes."

A moth fluttered near the lamp. He rose ghostlike, stalked

231

it, cornered it in the shadows of the far wall, and dispatched it.

"Congratulations," Joan said from her bent pillow and watched him undo his shirt. "What are you doing?"

"I'm going to bed. Do you mind moving over?"

Strangely, she didn't.

He opened his eyes and saw that he was alone. The sun was up, but he knew it was still early. It took him an ungodly long time to get out of the bed, for his game leg had stiffened diabolically. There was a large bathroom down the hall, and that was the one he hobbled to, the shower stall hot and vapory from recent use. After he stepped out of it, a towel knotted around his middle, he used a Lady's Remington on his face, but it pulled at more whiskers than it shaved. A packaged toothbrush lay near the sink. It seemed to have been placed there for him.

Later, his leg loosening, he made his way downstairs and found Joan in the kitchen. Her hair was severely brushed, but she was dressed in jersey and shorts as if for a day on the beach. "Are the others still in bed?" he asked with a certain deference, and she turned to him slowly.

"I wanted Pam out of the house for a while. Laura took her for a drive."

"This early?"

"They didn't sleep," Joan said a little sharply. She was tense, edgy. She opened the refrigerator and said distractedly, "There's no milk for cereal. We need milk."

"I'll go to Philpott's."

"It's not open yet."

The chief looked at his naked wrist and then at the wall clock. "Yes, it is."

He plodded across the boulevard to Philpott's, where the

early breakfast crowd lined the snack bar. He knew he looked shaggy and tried to avoid contact, but the man with the bicycle clips grasped his sleeve. The man had a quip to make, a near-insult to squeeze out, but the chief was in no mood to listen and pushed the hand away.

On his way down the aisle he picked up a throw-away razor and at the end of the aisle snatched up a gallon jug of milk. On the way back the man wearing the clips was waiting, something rehearsed on his tongue, a busy hand at his face, but before he could speak the chief said loudly, "Save it."

He paid for his purchases quickly, not waiting for change, and got out of the store fast but not far. Ed Robertshaw stood in his way, the bald head thrust forward. Color surged into Robertshaw's face.

"I told Alice I wanted to see you. You never showed up."

"I've been busy," the chief said without fear. "I'm still busy."

Robertshaw's eyes burned. "You set Wilbur Cox up. Your own sergeant."

"You don't know that."

"Damn you. You're playing God."

"You've been doing that for years."

"I'm different. I'm bigger than you. My people made this town and I'm carrying on. I'm the power here, Paul, *not you!*"

The chief offered no response and showed no concern. He merely shifted the milk jug to his other hand.

"I want your badge, Paul. At the next selectmen's meeting I want to see you lay it on the table. I'll personally pick it up."

"You can't make me do that," the chief said dispassionately. "I'm afraid not ever."

"No? Why not?"

"I know too much." Then the chief turned with a light step and crossed the boulevard cornerwise, cars slowing for him. For some reason his leg had quit hurting, at least for the time being. When he entered the gray house he heard the telephone ringing. Joan, who was standing in the kitchen almost where he had left her, was not bothering to answer it, as if she knew it was for him. "Shall I?" he asked, and she nodded.

It was his mother-in-law.

"I know where you are, Paul. Leo told me." Alice Cross's voice was a little dry, detached, level. "Do you have a girlfriend, Paul? You could have told me. Did you think I wouldn't understand?" She breathed in a way to let him know she was disappointed, and she absorbed his silence with a sigh. "I know three women are renting that place. Which one do you fancy? It must be the blonde. Linda would've looked like her if she'd lived."

"No," the chief said, "not that one."

"Maybe you'll tell me sometime."

"Yes, maybe," he said.

"When are you coming in, Paul?"

"When I get there," he said and gently hung up.

Joan had her back to him. When she turned and saw his face, she said, "You look worried."

"No," he said. "My mother-in-law is. She thinks I'm in love."

After they finished eating cereal, the chief went into the downstairs bathroom and shaved. He gazed hard into the mirror with each stroke. His face seemed oddly different to him, as if he were seeing parts of it for the first time. When he returned to the kitchen, Joan said, "I won't say you look like a new man, but you do look better." He smiled at her without commenting on her appearance. Her face was drawn and her eyes circled. She said, "You mustn't think we hate men, not even deep down, just those who have soiled us."

"What would have happened," he asked quietly, "if someone else had been blamed for something you three had done. Charged and convicted."

"Not convicted. I'd have played my ace."

"I figured that."

"Then why'd you ask?"

"I wanted to hear you say it."

They went out onto the beach, which was glazed with the morning wet, another sun-filled day. Joan wore a gray T-shirt over bright shorts. The chief walked with his shirt open.

She said, "We didn't know each other, not till later. We met Roger separately, you see. A handsome and intelligent man, seemingly sensitive, caring, totally charming. He looked a bit like Robert Lowell, but in a sleeker sort of way. He was very proud of his body, lean and elongated, supple, an El Greco creation. Can you picture that, Chief?"

"No."

"You don't want to. I don't either. I met him at a party he crashed. Laura was introduced to him at a church singles club. Pamela met him at a concert. He was such a smooth operator, and we were ridiculously easy prey. Divorce can be devastating, you see, the rejection unbearable. Roger would have made a wonderful shrink. He knew all the right things to say. He knew his Lowell. Lowell wheedled his way into posterity, Roger into us."

They skirted children with pails and shovels, some throwing sand. The sky seemed close, the blue pressing down. The chief said, "How did he hurt you?"

"Do you need the sordid details? The man was a sadist and despised women. When Laura finally refused to lend him any more money he poured lighter fluid on her and struck a match. It was only to scare her, but she didn't know that. Afterwards he pushed part of a mop handle up her rectum. There was considerable damage, and she went through surgery twice."

Before asking his next question, the chief looked away for a second. "What did he do to you?"

She shrugged. "I took some bad beatings, but he couldn't damage me any more than I was. It was about that time I learned I had cancer."

"How did you three get together?"

"Pam's doing. Roger carelessly left behind his little address book, our names in it, the rest from New York, where I guess he'd been living before, though that was not what he'd told us. He had different stories for each of us. Anyway, Pam rang up Laura and then me. We agreed to meet for drinks. Just to exchange horror stories. I remember it was at the Ritz, and it soon became apparent we all wanted him dead. It was an idea that grew. God, did it grow!"

The chief threw her a fast look as he scuffed sand. The sand got into his boot. Joan's lonely face half smiled.

"We wanted revenge, Chief, clear and simple. But we also wanted to stop him from mutilating any more women. No more victims. We decided that. Do you know what a victim is, Chief? Garbage. That's what we felt like."

"Who killed him? Who fired the pistol?"

"Do you really need to know?"

"I'd like to."

"Then I leave that to your imagination."

Ahead of them a young couple with a camera strayed apart for pictures. The man snapped several of the woman, opulent in her bathing suit. The chief and Joan passed in silence. Near the surf a mother skinned off her tiny son's playsuit and let him splash in the buff.

"I phoned him," Joan said. "I told him all was forgiven if only he'd please come back. He was suspicious, but so cocksure and arrogant he came anyway. He found the three of us waiting, music playing. I remember the smell of the cordite. Pam went a little hysterical afterward. Not because of what had been done but because of how absurdly easy it had been. The gun belonged to Laura. Her husband had carried it on civil rights marches. She was supposed to get rid of it, but Pam wanted it. It was her protection."

The chief, faintly haunted, gave a backwards glance almost like a fugitive fearing a hound had picked up his scent. They began walking closer to the surf, where wave-riding gulls viewed them with seeming disdain. "The body," the chief said. "What did you do with it?"

"Pam had a station wagon back then, and we drove to a town in Connecticut that Laura knew about. Don't ask me how we managed. I honestly don't remember. I just know we got him into the car and out of it and pushed his body into a marsh near a chemical plant. Laura said the water was highly acidic."

The beach turned pebbly, fewer people. Joan stopped dead in her tracks, dramatically, but it was only to fasten a strap on her sandal. Her hands shook.

"Do you want to know about the dentist? We had a good idea what kind of man he was, and we tried to avoid him, which only spurred him on. He couldn't believe that any unattached woman wasn't interested in his company. In Philpott's he rubbed against Laura and me, and we turned on him. He pretended it was an accident. Later he did the same thing to Pam, except she froze, and he thought that was her way of being receptive. Then he started bothering her on the beach and in the water. He never jogged on the beach late at night until somehow he discovered that was when she went jogging. He stalked her. He cornered her near those boulders, and she simply did what she did before. She froze. She could not bear the thought of being beat up again. What he did was ravish a zombie."

Gulls alighted nearby and arrayed themselves as if for a charge. The chief slowly stepped over a sand dollar that looked newly minted and waited for her to go on.

"She knew he'd be back sometime. Three nights she waited for him near the boulders. The third night it was terribly dark, but she knew it was him. She said she could smell him."

"She shot him."

The steps were desultory. A youth approached from the opposite direction, his gait brisk, his head taken up with a pirate's red bandanna. In passing he gave them a friendly greeting, and they nodded like a married couple, Joan with the start of a smile, as if the youth, though a little younger, reminded her of her son. She pressed a hand to her brow.

"I'm tired," she said. "Tired of talking about it."

"I don't need to know about the boating instructor, only Lyman Arnold."

"He was drunk."

"I know that," the chief pressed, "but tell me about it anyway. Did he come back after the party?"

"Laura and I had gone to bed. Pam couldn't sleep and was cleaning up downstairs. He must've poked a stick through the screen door to lift the latch. Laura woke me. She had dug the gun out of Pam's room and told me that something was wrong downstairs. We crept down there. Pam lay under him with a fist jammed in her mouth. I don't think he saw that, and now I don't even think he thought he was raping her, she was so passive, a terrible pattern she had gotten into."

The chief said, "You don't have to finish."

"You asked, I'll tell you. He leaped up when he saw us. I'm not even sure now that Laura meant to shoot. I thought she missed because he didn't fall. He just had a shocked look on his face. Then he was terrified. He didn't know it, but so were we. He stumbled and bolted through the door. He leaped off the porch, and then we saw him running down the beach. We saw him go into the ocean. We stayed on the porch the rest of the night, and we never saw him come out."

The chief stopped in his tracks and stood like sculpture. "What are you doing?"

"Resting."

She gazed in one direction and then another. There was no one around in seeing distance. Without his noticing, she reached into the rear pocket of her shorts, a small bulge there. Her hand flinched before she bared the pistol. She didn't point it. She merely held it carelessly, and the chief stared at it, his brow furrowed.

"Is it loaded?"

"There's a bullet left."

"You could have used it on me last night, after the wine."

"There was never a question of that."

"Perhaps you'd better give it to me."

"Perhaps I had."

After she passed it over, he balanced it in his palm, his chin lifted, as if he actually had not wanted to touch it. "What makes you think this will end anything?"

"We've all agreed it can't go on. This weekend Pam wants to fly to Seattle to try to work out reconciliation with her children, especially her daughter. Laura used to be a counselor at her husband's church. She's willing to go along to help. If Pam gets her kids back, she would never jeopardize that relationship."

"What if she doesn't get them back?"

"Laura will be there to look after her."

"Do they know about you yet?"

"Not yet. They think I've worked something out with you. I've been waiting for you to tell if that's true."

Staring at gulls feathering low over the waves, he said, "How long do you have?"

"Not long. The marijuana doesn't help anymore." Then she gazed off at the ocean as if curiously excited by the imminence of her own death. The chief's lean shadow swept past her. "What are you doing?"

The tide spumed in. Salt spray stained his chinos, and the sand melted under his feet. He reared up and with all his might hurled the pistol into the distance, where for a split second it seemed suspended in the air, frozen in time. Then it plunged into the whitecaps.

It was a silent trek back. Many new faces were on the beach, eyes staring out of sunburns. They were people who rented for the month, not the season. Some he recognized, many he did not, though he was already memorizing them. "There's your friend," Joan murmured as they neared the gray house, and, shielding his eyes, he glimpsed Winnie Wallace poised near the fuchsia. When they climbed the porch steps, Winnie glided forward to meet them. She was crisply dressed, silver-gray curls all in place. She scrutinized him and then smiled mysteriously at Joan.

"Paul and I go way back. High school. He used to kiss me till my mouth was sore, didn't you, Paul?"

"Yes," he said. "As a matter of fact I did. What do you want, Winnie?"

"I'll leave you two alone," Joan said and slipped into the house. He caught sight of Pamela at one of the windows, her face solemnly calm, as if certain guilts and fears had been carried since he last saw her. Then she stepped back and thinned away. He did not see Laura, only her shadow.

Winnie drifted back to the fuchsia, picked at it, and said, "They're leaving, you know. I wonder if they'll give this to me."

"What are you doing here, Winnie?"

"Your mother-in-law phoned. Ironic, isn't it? Alice calling me. She wanted to know if I knew what you were doing here. Then do you know what she asked me? When are we going to get married? She wants you married, Paul, and the queer thing is she suddenly wants me to be the bride, maybe because I'm a known quantity, no surprises."

"What did you say?"

"I told her it was too late. That's what you wanted me to say, isn't it?"

He said nothing. He seemed to have had vitality a moment ago but little now. Down on the beach the lifeguard blew his whistle. A youth was swimming out too far, and the chief thought how lucky the kid was to have someone draw him back.

He felt Winnie's eyes focusing hard on him. Blue eyes faded. Hers hadn't yet. She said, "You've done a good thing, Paul. I shouldn't be surprised, but I am."

"How much do you know?"

"No more than you want me to."

From somewhere inside the house came the sound of a door closing. A window shade breathed against a screen. His mind's eye conjured up a naked length of thigh, but he was not sure whose it was.

"Well," Winnie said with a sudden forced laugh, "I've got to get back to work. I've sold a house on Robandy Road, did I tell you?"

"Wait a minute," he said and followed her down the steps.

Twenty-four

It was a brisk day in October when he heard about it. He was breakfasting at Philpott's and half listening to two old men argue over a baseball game played more than fifty years ago. For them the players were still alive, still functioning on the field, still adding to their statistics. He was on the verge of ordering another cup of coffee when the clerk at the cash register called out to him.

"You want to take this, Chief? I think it's your girlfriend."

He made his way slowly past the aisles and by the time he put the phone to his ear he had divined what Winnie would tell him.

". . . last night, three days after she checked into Mass General."

"Who called you?" he asked. "Mrs. Comeau?"

"Yes, how did you know?"

A few minutes later he crossed the boulevard and, without looking at the gray house, ambled down the beach. The day was overcast, the sea one with the sky. Waves cracked against the sand. Hetty Nelson, bundled in a great ragged sweater and helmeted in a knit cap, was poking about near the boulders. "I thought you'd want to know," he said and told her about Joan's death. For a long moment the old woman's eyes remained blank. Then they sparked.

"That was my chum."

"Yes," the chief said, "mine too."

Later, alone with Winnie in her kitchen, coffee perking, he

242

inquired about a memorial service, and Winnie gave a small shrug. "I don't know, Paul. Probably in Cambridge."

"One of us should go."

"I don't think we're wanted," she countered quietly and rested her chin on the back of her fist. Then softly she began asking him questions he was not prepared to answer, at least not aloud, not yet. "If you loved her, it's all right," she said. "You can tell me."

"I had a few feelings for her, that's all."

"If you want to fool yourself, Paul, that's okay. And if you don't want to marry me, that's okay, too."

"You're wrong. I do."

It was a raw morning in late November, no sun showing, when Joan emerged from her apartment building in Cambridge, and the chief approached her with a dark sense of rediscovery. She stood shadowy, immobile, unperturbed, while he shivered. He was wearing a lined windbreaker and a sweater beneath, but the cold cut through his chinos. She had on a fitted cashmere coat and suede boots, her hair gathered under a stylish felt hat. Her smile was convincingly casual and impeccably proper as she gave a little look at her watch. She was still a publicist for the museum and had a breakfast appointment at the Ritz. The chief, his eyes full of her, said, "You look healthy as a horse."

"That's the nicest thing anybody could say to me," she said, perfectly cool. A cab pulled up. It was for her and she signaled the driver to wait a moment. The chief stood rodlike.

"You conned me."

"You wanted me to."

"No."

"Yes."

The chief's face took on a sad look. The traffic on her street was heavy, and the fumes were giving him a headache. "You never had cancer."

"Test results suggested it. And the pain was real."

"What was it?"

"An ulcer, among other things."

"You knew it. On the beach you knew it. You could have told me."

"You were proud of the way you figured everything out, and I didn't want to take anything away from you." She smiled faintly, with bright lips. The cabby sounded his horn, and she gestured for more time with an imperious wave of her hand.

The chief said, "I was good to you."

"I'd never argue with that."

"Then why the final con? The call from Mrs. Comeau." His eyes bored into her. "It wasn't necessary."

"I wanted to wrap it up for you, in your own mind. But your mind quit playing the game."

"I had to come here. That's what you didn't want. You were afraid I'd bother you. You don't trust any man do you?"

"That's the answer, Chief. I'm sorry."

The cabbie heaved an exaggerated sigh of relief as they approached. The chief opened the door for her, closed it behind her, and peered in through the half-open window, his hand on the edge. She nodded at his wedding ring.

"Congratulations."

The following summer they booked rooms for July and a part of August in a small seaside inn in Kennebunkport, Maine. Laura lay in the sun and read *The World According to Garp*. When the tide was out Pamela explored offshore rocks, where seals were sometimes seen. Joan made friends with two elderly sisters and often walked with them along the surf in the late afternoon. Each day was no different from the other, which was what they wanted, but the third week turned ugly. In the tiny bar inside the inn they watched a man heave a drink into a woman's face. The woman, his wife, pretended it had been a joke and groped blindly for a napkin. The man inched it out of her reach.

The next day they saw him on the beach, or rather he saw them. He sought them out. They lay long and flat on bright towels, and he, beetle-browed, crouched near them in brilliant swim trunks and let the hot sand breathe up his calves. The usual things came out of his mouth. They tried to ignore him. They swung onto their sides, their backs to him, which in no way discouraged him. Finally Pamela turned her sun-scathed face toward him, shoved the blond hair from her eyes, and said, "Piss off."

It didn't work. He scooped sand and made a hole. They got to their feet. They moved with purpose, their strides synchronized in military fashion, toward the rhythmic roar of high tide and the sharp angles of the waves.

Laura said grimly, "He's classic. Another Roger."

Joan said, "He's digging his own grave."